Cherry

Shelley Munro

Munro Press

Cherry

Print ISBN: 978-1-99-106367-0
Ebook ISBN: 978-0-9951395-1-0

Editor: Evil Eye Editing
Cover: Kim Killion, The Killion Group, Inc.

Munro Press, New Zealand.

First Munro Press electronic publication October 2020
First Munro Press print publication November 2024

DEDICATION

For Paul, my husband, partner in crime, and fellow adventurer.
Every day is a good day.

Introduction

Love is a mystery, but dragons are real.

Cherry is gutted when her friend Liza disappears, presumed drowned. She has no time to mourn, however, since she must keep Liza's daughter safe from Liza's ex. Cherry sneaks away to Holy Island, where she meets a big, sexy, tattooed man washed up on the beach. A big, sexy, *deluded* man since he insists he's a dragon.

Accused of a crime he didn't commit, Martinos has escaped the dungeon only to wash up on the mainland. Returning to the Dragon Isles is not his most immediate problem, though, since his dragon is bound, and he cannot shift.

Unlucky in love, Cherry is surprised when Martinos returns her growing lust and camaraderie. While the man has a flawed mind, he's excellent with Liza's daughter and not one of Cherry's internal alarms ping. With Martinos, her life is stimulating, and she's falling for him. Then, everything she thought she understood about dragons pops like a balloon, and her real adventure begins.

You will love this second book in the Dragon Isles trilogy because it introduces a courageous and curvy human, a sexy dragon suffering

1

through hell through no fault of his own, and an unfamiliar world full of mystery, magic, and mayhem. Plus one or two dragon-caused incidents when tempers race out of control.

Author's Note

The idea behind the Dragon Isles series was two-fold. First, I spotted a pre-made cover designed by . It featured a woman with a land and sea view behind her. The clouds above were in the shape of a dragon, and the title was *The Mystery of Dragon Island*. I fell in love with the cover and purchased it even though I didn't have a story ready to go with it.

Many months later, I was watching one of my favorite programs, *Escape to the Country*. They always have a special interest item on the show, and the particular one I saw was about Newcastle Emlyn, the village where the last dragon in Wales supposedly died. I immediately thought of my cover, waiting for its story and blended the two ideas.

This trilogy wasn't a story that came easily. The three books are interconnected, and I struggled to pull the threads together. But I'm stubborn and determined, and although I grappled with my characters and plot, the romances proved the perfect way to occupy myself during our COVID lockdown here in New Zealand.

The setting

I adore England, and it's like coming home each time I visit. The story concept I visualized suited an English setting, but deciding where to place my islands took a long time. To those readers who live in Northumberland or those who are familiar with the area, please forgive me. I have played fast and loose with the geography of the region. Some of my setting is real and is what you'll find in the area while in other places, I've used artistic license. My story has cliffs, but in reality, the area is much flatter. I have placed trees where there are none, and Lindisfarne Castle is furnished in the Edwardian style as it was during the period Edward Hudson owned it as a holiday home.

Just go with it, okay? Enjoy the romance, and please forgive me for my writer's imagination because I couldn't find everything I needed in the way of a setting to keep things real.

I hope you enjoy the adventure and soar with the dragons, and please subscribe to my newsletter if you'd like to keep up with my upcoming releases and news.

(https://shelleymunro.com/newsletter/)

Shelley

CHAPTER 1

Liza Disappears and Cherry Flees

C herry Lawford grinned as she listened to Liza Carrington rave over the panoramic view. Her best friend was driving along the coast after a trip to interview a couple in a small Northumberland village.

"I have the top down, and the wind is blowing in my hair. It's such a gorgeous day. I can see Lindisfarne in the distance. You know—Holy Island. We should visit the island one day soon." Liza's voice sounded distant because she was using her speakerphone while driving.

"We can have a Tony-free weekend since the crossing over to the island depends on the tide. Imagine. Any drama will be of our own making."

"And here I am, stuck in the bookstore," Cherry said.

"You love your books and your store," Liza countered, her affectionate tone curving Cherry's lips to another smile. "It's one of my favorite places."

"I'm up for a weekend trip. Mum won't mind filling in for me for two days. You're right. We deserve a break from your ex. I can't believe the dick move he pulled at Joanna's school."

"I'm not surprised." Liza blew out a frustrated sigh, her irritation transparent even though they couldn't see each other. "Tony is escalating after I categorically refused to pay him off. I mean, if I cave and give him cash, what's stopping him from approaching me for more in six months? He wasn't capable of holding onto money during our marriage. I doubt he's changed."

"Why won't he sign the divorce papers? I don't get it," Cherry said.

"He lives to mess up my life," Liza said, this time her tone one of defeat. "I—popsicles!"

"What's happening? What's wrong?" Cherry demanded at the awed note in her friend's voice. "Liza, talk to me."

The next second, Liza screamed. The screech of metal against metal squealed down the phone line. Alarm roared through Cherry, a burst of adrenaline, and her pulse raced in a gallop.

"Liza? What's happening? Liza!"

Their call cut off without warning, and through her panic, Cherry saw spots in front of her eyes. She disconnected to still the *beep-beep-beep* of her phone and redialed Liza.

Nothing happened.

The phone rang and rang and rang.

Liza didn't answer.

Cherry gripped her phone, staring at the screen and willing it to sing in her Robin Hood ringtone. A businessman wove through her store seating area and placed a bestselling novel and a self-help book on the counter. She rang up the sale and sent the customer on his way with a forced smile.

Cherry locked the door of her bookstore and flipped the open sign to closed. That done, she darted to her phone and called Rena, Liza's half-sister.

"What's up?" Rena asked, her mind obviously elsewhere.

"Liza! I was talking to her. She screamed, and it sounded as if she crashed. I tried calling, but the phone is dead on her end."

"Where was she?" Rena sounded more alert.

"Heading back from her last dragon interview. She drove the coast road to enjoy the sun and sea breeze."

"Call emergency services while I collect Joanna from school." Rena snapped out instructions in her usual take-charge way.

"What about Tony?"

"I spoke with the headmistress. She's watching Joanna until I arrive. The headmistress told me to park in the rear staff car park."

"All right. Bring Joanna here. If Tony is pissed, he'll loiter at Liza's cottage. He won't come here straightaway, and by that time, we might've heard from Liza."

"Have a pot of tea waiting," Rena ordered. "I'm not sleeping well. Weird dreams."

"You can tell me when you get here," Cherry said. "I'll ring Liza again before I contact the cops."

Cherry disconnected, and her hand shook as she tried Liza's phone. Nothing. Someone knocked on the door, but Cherry ignored her prospective customer and rang emergency services, a coldness prickling across her skin and tears smarting her eyes.

"It's my friend," she said. "She's had an accident."

An hour later, she opened her shop door to Rena and Joanna and led the way up the stairs to the second level and to the compact kitchen. While she was waiting for news—any news—she'd made sandwiches and arranged biscuits on a plate. She boiled the kettle and poured the water into her china teapot.

"Joanna, a glass of milk today, or do you prefer juice?"

"Milk, please, Aunt Cherry."

As always, Joanna's sweet voice calling her *Aunt* mushed Cherry's insides and tightened an invisible band around her chest. She'd always wanted children. Her fiancé hadn't. Cherry had hoped to change his mindset, but he'd stood firm.

Shoving away the past, she reached for a glass and filled it with milk.

"There you go, poppet. How was school today?"

"Bradley pulled my ponytail."

Rena rolled her eyes. "Do boys still do that shi...ah, stuff?"

"He had scissors," Joanna informed her aunt, full of indignation. "Mrs. Canter shouted at him."

Cherry restrained her inappropriate grin. "I hope he got a detention."

Joanna's head bobbed, setting her ponytail in motion. "A big one. His best friend, too. Sam got in trouble for pushing Evelyn. Her knees were bleeding."

Rena rolled her eyes, a tsking sound whistling through her teeth. "What is wrong with parents these days? They're raising little monsters." She helped herself to a sandwich and bit with an appreciative moan. "Yum! Ham and mustard. My favorite."

Cherry stared at her watch. The police constable had promised to contact her by four. It was after that now. She rose on shaky legs. "Back in a few minutes. I have to make a call." *And hear excellent news.* She crossed her fingers before glancing at Rena and trying to communicate everything she felt and feared in that one look. "We'll talk then."

Amid her bookshelves—the self-help section and the top one hundred fiction—Cherry worked her throat, a stupid lump damming her voice. She hit return call.

"Police Constable Merrick speaking."

"Yes, it's Cherry Lawford here. You told me to ring you for news of my friend."

The constable took an audible breath. "Ms. Lawford, you indicated your friend drove a red car. We've discovered a broken roadside railing and flakes of red paint."

Cherry pressed her free hand to her chest and leaned against a shelf to bolster her shaky knees. "Liza?"

"I've called in a dive team from the nearest town. The wind is whipping up the waves, and the conditions have deteriorated this afternoon. The divers will investigate first thing in the morning." He paused, the pregnant silence full of kindness and unspoken sympathy. "I'm sorry the news isn't better."

A sob burst from Cherry. "W-where...um...did my friend...the accident happen?"

"I'm sorry," the policeman said.

"Where on the coastal road?"

"Close to the Lindisfarne causeway," the constable said.

"I...thank you. You'll ring if—"

"The moment we have information," the constable promised.

"Thanks," she whispered, unable to push out another word. She disconnected, and tears shrouded her vision. She sniffed and knuckled away the moisture.

Keep yourself together.

No point in upsetting Joanna. Not yet.

Mask your emotions. You can do this. For Liza and Joanna. She brushed away a tear that spilled onto her cheek and shuffled up the stairs and back to the small kitchenette, immeasurably older under the ominous burden.

Cartoon voices spilled from the television in her snug, and Rena appeared in the doorway.

"I know you don't approve of television for kids, but I'm going crazy with not knowing what's happening. Did the police find Liza?"

Cherry shook her head, not trusting herself to speak.

"Tell me everything from the beginning," Rena demanded.

Cherry sniffed and reached for a tissue from a travel packet she kept in her handbag. "I was talking to Liza, and she told me she was driving along the coast road. In the middle of our conversation, she saw something, then screamed. The local cop checked the road. He didn't locate Liza but discovered a spot where a vehicle had breached the guardrail. They found flakes of red paint." She swallowed hard. "He didn't say it, but he implied Liza drove off the cliff."

"Any sign of her car?" Rena's poker face signaled she didn't care and was merely showing polite interest. Cherry knew better.

"A dive team is going to the spot tomorrow morning."

"Why can't they go now?" Rena checked her wristwatch. "It's summer and light for hours yet."

"The sea is too rough. It's not safe."

"Holy f-frogs," Rena spluttered.

They tried not to swear around Joanna, determined to set an

exemplary example.

Cherry sniffed and swiped at yet another escapee tear. "What should we do? We have to tell Joanna something. She expects Liza home tonight. And Tony? When this hits the news, he'll try to grab Joanna. As Joanna's father, he has more rights than us."

Rena frowned, lines digging deep into her forehead. She yawned without warning, slapping her hand across her mouth a fraction too late. Now that Cherry focused on Rena, she spotted the shadows her makeup failed to conceal.

"Joanna can stay here with me," Cherry said.

"That won't work. Not for long. Tony followed me from the school. He was furious because we whisked away Joanna."

Cherry grimaced, her mind racing with the obstacles Tony might throw in their way. Her friend had sounded so carefree. Happy in a way she hadn't revealed for months. She'd moved on as much as she could while dragging Tony's bullshit behind her. Tears spilled over Cherry's cheeks.

"Please stop," Rena said in a plaintive voice. "If you cry, I'll start. We need to hold it together for Joanna, at least until we have solid info from the cops."

"The policeman told me the accident occurred near Holy Island or at least the turnoff to the causeway."

"That's weird," Rena said.

Cherry plucked another tissue from her handbag. She blew her nose.

"What's weird?"

"Doesn't Holy Island have an old abbey? I've been dreaming of an abbey and a man in a robe for the last two weeks. That's why I look so haggard. My sleep isn't restful."

She paused, and Cherry watched a hint of pink climb into Rena's cheeks.

"What aren't you saying?" Cherry asked. "You're blushing."

"Ah, the man walks into my room and shrugs off his robe. He's naked. Dream me holds out my arms in invitation, and he climbs into my bed. You'd imagine a monk wears a robe to hide a skinny physique and knobby knees. My robed man is built. He's strong and muscled and has these weird blue tattoos on his arms and chest. He kisses me, starts making love, and let's just say the man has skills. I have the most amazing climax, but every single time I wake, the sexual tension almost breaks me. A battery-operated boyfriend is not doing the job."

Cherry sighed. "Join the club. I'd appreciate even a sex dream to get me revved."

"Thought you were going out with James or Jim. Whatever his name."

"Tim. And no. He told me there was no spark. His mother informed him love is a magical thing, and he's not feeling it with me."

Rena snorted. "Any adult male who lives with his mother is best avoided."

"I hear you." Cherry heaved out a miserable sigh. "Popsicles, what should we tell Joanna?"

"Nothing at the moment. If she asks, we'll say Liza had to overnight at the village where the last dragon died. We'll tell Joanna Liza needed to do more research for her dragon book."

Cherry gulped. "Okay. We'll learn more tomorrow, I guess. Are you telling your father?"

"He's in Los Angeles for a business meeting. If he calls, I'll tell him, but otherwise, I'll wait for details. It's not as if we can make decisions right now."

"Oh, heck! It's my fault. I shouldn't have called her."

"She didn't need to answer. Liza could've pulled over to take your call. Besides, doesn't she use her hands-free?"

Cherry sniffed and searched for another tissue. "Yes, but that doesn't make me feel less guilty."

For the rest of the evening, Cherry ran through the motions while wearing an upbeat mood for Joanna. After Rena left, Cherry cooked fish fingers, oven chips, and peas for Joanna's supper.

"Mum never told me she was staying in the dragon village," Joanna said after swallowing a mouthful of peas. Her brown gaze speared Cherry, and Cherry bit her lip to stem a babble of unnecessary details.

Instead, Cherry reached for her glass of wine. If she kept her mouth busy, she couldn't blurt extra explanations.

She'd always hated secrets.

Preferred to tell the truth.

"She was excited to visit this village." *Truth*. "She wanted to gather extra information for her book." *Fact*.

"But it's my art show tomorrow at school. Will she be back in time to see my pictures? I have two projects in the show."

"I'm not sure." *Truth*. "Did you mention the art show?"

Joanna's lip shot out in a pout. "I forgot."

"Well, I'll send a text and hope the message reaches her." *Also, the truth*. Cherry intended to pray hard, even though she wasn't a religious person.

Tony had cheated on her friend and hounded her after he'd followed Liza to England from New Zealand. Reading between the lines, Cherry suspected Tony had hit Liza too. No way he loved his daughter. The man used her as a tool to lever Liza into submission. He craved money, loathe to let Liza walk without earning his payday. The man was a bastard. Handsome and charming when it suited him, but still a mean scoundrel. Cherry had no compunction in lying to Tony and messing with his plans to jerk around Liza. It was her twisting of truth with Joanna that bothered her more.

"Can we ring her?" Joanna asked.

"We can try, but the telephone reception is spotty where your mother is staying tonight."

Joanna stabbed her fork into her remaining fish finger. "Okay."

Please, Liza. Please come home to us. Cherry took another sip of wine and sent yet another prayer winging skyward.

Liza hadn't died. She couldn't have.

The next morning, Cherry helped Joanna prepare for school. She tugged a comb through Joanna's chocolate brown curls. "Which hairstyle for today?"

"Something important? For our art show."

"I suggest either a braid or a bun at the back of your neck. A bun will stop the boys from messing with your hair again."

"Yes," Joanna said decisively. "None of my friends ever have buns."

Cherry combed and twisted and pinned, then pulled a red scrunchie over the top to hold her hair construction in place. "There you go. How does that look?" She held a mirror for Joanna to inspect her hairstyle.

"Ooh!" Joanna beamed and clapped her hands. "Cool! It's perfect, Aunt Cherry."

Relief struck Cherry. She'd added a slice of happiness to the girl's day. "My work here is done, poppet. Let's have breakfast, then we'll get you to school."

So far, Cherry had heard nothing from the local police station. She'd rung and left a terse message to call her as soon as possible. The police hadn't contacted Rena either, but Tony had left several angry diatribes. It was his weekend for Joanna, and he'd wanted to pick her up a day early.

The ring of a doorbell told Cherry of Rena's arrival. At least, she hoped it was Rena. She pulled a box of cornflakes out of the cupboard and reached into another cabinet to grab a dessert bowl.

"Joanna, take a seat and pour out the cornflakes into your bowl."

"Yes, Aunt Cherry."

As Cherry had suspected, Joanna jumped at the chance to complete an adult task.

The bell rang again for longer this time. Cherry opened the door once she'd confirmed it was Rena.

"Any news?" Cherry asked.

"I rang the number you gave me and got the answerphone message. Tony, however, is a real arse-hole. He has blown up my phone with messages and texts, and in the last few, he threatened to call the cops on Liza if she doesn't hand over Joanna. What should we do?"

"We can't cave to Tony. He doesn't love Joanna."

"We need to drive past the accident site. Maybe we'll learn something."

A sob burst from Cherry, and she pressed her lips together to stem the sound. She reached into her pocket and pulled out a hanky to dab her eyes before she focused on Rena. "But that will mean telling Joanna the truth. That her mother is missing, presumed d-dead."

Rena closed the distance between them and embraced Cherry. "No one knows for sure. Don't borrow trouble."

"The cop didn't sound hopeful when I spoke with him last

night."

"Did he say that?" Rena asked.

"It was what he didn't say. He implied Liza had drowned."

"We're not sure," Rena repeated. "We're assuming."

Cherry mopped up her tears and blew her nose. Joanna couldn't see her this way. Liza counted on her and Rena to care for Joanna, and Cherry refused to fail her friend. "Any idea of how to escape town without Tony realizing what's happening? We're lucky the accident hasn't hit the news yet."

"I had another dream last night."

A trace of impatience stabbed Cherry in the chest. "We don't have time for sex dreams."

"This one was different. Robe Guy told me to give you a message."

"What? *Me?*" Cherry realized her mouth had dropped open, and she pressed her lips together in a flat line.

"He told me my friend Cherry would meet a man on Holy Island. A stranger on the beach and that you should help him."

"That's interesting..." Cherry said in an understatement. Crazy. *Rena was completely crazy.*

"I'm passing on his message," Rena said, her manner almost defensive.

Cherry opened her mouth to ask more questions when Joanna appeared at the top of the stairs.

"Aunt Cherry, I'm gonna be late for school. I'm hungry, and I spilled the milk. It's dripping off the table."

Cherry whirled and jogged up to the second level—her accommodation above her bookstore. She rushed into her kitchenette and dived into action since Joanna looked tearful.

"Is this where I say no crying over spilled milk?" Rena asked, having followed Cherry.

Cherry bit back a chuckle. "No problem, Joanna. Did you get milk on your dress?"

"N-no."

"Love your hair. Very stylish," Rena said to Joanna in an apparent diversion. "I know today is your art show, but what if we took you on an adventure before we meet your mother? Aunt Cherry can show you how to make a beach collage. That way you can hold a private art show for us."

"Rena," Cherry said in stark warning. The police suspected the worst and, given what she'd heard, Cherry thought their assumptions close to the truth. Rena couldn't make promises to her niece.

"You didn't let me finish my dream story. You'll meet the stranger and should help him. He won't hurt you but will protect you. The other part of my dream was of an island where dragons lived," Rena said. "Somehow, Robe Guy waved his hand and showed me a picture. Liza was there on the island with the dragons."

"You told me you couldn't understand what he was trying to

say," Cherry whispered. "Don't make promises we can't keep." She poured cornflakes into another bowl and added milk for Joanna.

"Will we see a dragon?" Joanna asked.

"No," Cherry said.

"Yes," Rena contradicted.

"Rena," Cherry snapped. "You can't make promises."

"Aunt Cherry, I'll try to draw a dragon," Joanna said. "I could write a story like Mummy."

"Eat your cornflakes while I speak with Aunt Rena." Cherry grabbed Rena's arm and dragged her into the next room. "What the devil are you trying to do? You can't—this won't end well."

"Liza mentioned Holy Island, right? You told me that."

"She mentioned having a vacation there. A few days' break."

"We need to keep Joanna out of Tony's clutches. We can't afford to mess around with Tony snapping at our heels. Take Joanna and make a run for it today. I can borrow a child who will pass for Joanna at a distance. I'm convinced Tony followed me this morning. This might throw him off the scent and fool him into thinking it's business as usual."

"And meanwhile?"

"You take Joanna to Holy Island. Check the internet to see when you can cross the causeway and stay there until Tony gives up."

"I don't know," Cherry said. "I can't close my store."

"Ask your mother to mind the bookstore," Rena said. "She's offered. I've heard her."

"She changes things," Cherry complained. "Mum can't do much damage in the hour or two she helps me, but a week or longer?" Cherry shuddered and lifted her hands in a dramatic gesture.

"Does it matter? Isn't it more important to help Joanna since Liza can't?"

Cherry considered Rena's suggestion and came closer to caving. "Are you sure we should do this? What if we contact your father?"

"I'll do that after Joanna is safe. When we hear from the police."

Cherry still hesitated. "What if Tony tells the cops I've kidnapped his daughter? You know he's capable of spinning a story."

"We need to stall until Liza can get to us."

Cherry gaped at Rena. "Are you listening to yourself?" She glanced at the door, knowing Joanna disliked missing school. "It looks as if Liza drove over a cliff. How can she still be alive?"

"She was alive in my dream."

"It was a dream, Rena."

"I know it sounds crazy, but it was so real. Look, give it two or three days. By that time, we'll have more info. If things don't turn out the way my dream showed, we'll come up with another plan. Dad should be back in England by then."

Cherry screwed her eyes shut, wanting to weep yet again. This was ridiculous. A horrible nightmare. Soon she'd wake. They'd have Liza at home, and her interfering mother would be the worst of Cherry's worries.

It wasn't a terrible dream. Cherry drove out of town, her gaze on her rear-vision mirror. So far, she hadn't spied Tony. Rena, true to her word, had drawn Tony away by pretending to take a Joanna lookalike to school.

"What's wrong, Aunt Cherry?" Joanna asked.

"I'm worried I forgot something important," Cherry fibbed. She was a terrible liar. Even Liza's daughter saw through her.

"When will we see Mum? I can't wait to show her my dragon story."

Cherry said nothing. She couldn't. The lump in her throat blocked her voice while her mind struggled with sorrow, sympathy, and ineffectual words that offered not a shred of comfort. With a shrug, she pushed a button, and the audio version of a *Harry Potter* book flowed into the silence.

"Yay!" Joanna said, clapping her hands. "It's the first book."

"Yes," Cherry croaked. She turned her attention to the road and the busy intersection ahead. Joanna reminded her of Liza so much. It was their mannerisms, the way they tilted their heads. While Liza's hair was straight, Joanna had inherited the deeper chocolate brown and a slight curl of her reprobate father. The one thing the man had going for him—he didn't need a paper bag to hide his head.

The nasty thought brought a rush of shame. Liza refused to speak ill of her ex in front of Joanna, and Cherry needed to subscribe to the same rule, even in her thoughts. Lord, what was she going to do without Liza?

Her friend was more outgoing and loved meeting people while Cherry hovered behind the scenes and sought refuge in her books. Her mother had always wondered aloud if purchasing the bookstore had been a suitable move for Cherry. But she'd met Liza and Rena because of her bookstore. The two women had dragged her out to lunch, to the corner pub, and the local nightclub, so Cherry's mother's complaints regarding her lack of a social life had faded.

Not the grandchild refrain, but baby steps.

The unintended pun had Cherry whooshing out a frustrated breath. As much as she loved her mother, she wished she'd stop spouting forth on kids and Cherry's lack of progress. Despite what her mother thought, she refused to settle. She wanted tall, dark, handsome, and kind, and she rejected any man who didn't make her heart go pitter-patter.

Too many romance novels, according to her mother, while Liza had informed her that tall, dark, and handsome didn't make the perfect partner.

"They need a personality and the drive to earn their way in life instead of expecting someone to hand it to them," Liza had said in a dry voice—one that spoke from experience.

Cherry pushed the topic to the rear of her mind and turned off the main highway. She'd chosen the coast road so she'd come across the police and their search. She glanced at Joanna, who listened to *Harry Potter*, and the burden on Cherry's shoulders had her slumping for an instant.

Liza—what should she tell Joanna?

She had no bloody idea.

CHAPTER 2

Freedom—Feel the Wind in My Beard

F rom the moment Martinos separated from Leo and Gwenyth, his skin itched as if his back bore a target proclaiming him an escapee. He sneaked through familiar back streets, relishing the puff of fresh air on his bearded face. He doubted many would recognize him with this bushy beard, his shoulder-length, matted black hair, and threadbare clothes. His feet were bare since the guards had relieved him of his expensive leather boots on his first day in captivity almost three years ago.

A commotion—a series of shouts and bangs sounded from behind him, and Martinos darted along the nearest alley and backed against a shadowed wall. Rooted to the spot, he blinked rapidly, his shoulders tight while he listened for his pursuers. The shouts increased, and his heart almost beat out of his chest. Then the thumps and crashes, the yells passed his hiding spot.

Acute relief had him slumping forward and releasing a ragged breath. It took him long moments to straighten and force his legs to hold his weight. These particular guards weren't chasing him. Martinos sidled to the alley exit and peered out in both directions. No one paid attention, so he shuffled from his hidey-hole and scuttled along the street toward the nearby forest.

With little exercise during his incarceration and barely enough food to keep him alive, this race to the human village promised to take its toll on him physically. Mentally... Well, he wasn't certain. There'd been months where he'd spoken to no one and conversed with himself since his dragon remained uncommunicative. He'd cursed his sister and his friends and muttered plans of revenge. Gwenyth's arrival had changed everything, and thanks to their quick friendship, he'd escaped. Determination gritted his jaw, and he pushed his legs to greater haste.

His breath soon emerged in raspy pants, the spear of pain beneath his rib cage squeezing a groan from him. He'd suspected his limited training and the exercises he'd done might have little effect, and this proved right. Too bad. He'd have to make do because he'd fight anyone who tried to return him to that cursed dungeon.

He hadn't raped the girl.

While he had no evidence of the culprit's identity, he held strong suspicions. But the reasons behind his imprisonment... He didn't have a single clue. The yearning for revenge ate at him, and the gloating visits from his sister had exacerbated his determination. He'd guessed she was part of the scheme to get rid of him when she refused to help him. Though why the dragons behind the plan hadn't killed him and ended the game puzzled him. Something else to investigate once he'd earned his freedom.

Leo had given him directions to the village, and Martinos's mood lightened on learning he hadn't lied. The fierce dragon had hated the friendliness between Martinos and Gwenyth, hadn't trusted him, yet he hadn't acted mean-spirited and directed Martinos straight back to capture.

Between the rooftops, he glimpsed thunders of guard dragons flying overhead. The impossibility of escape was enough to make him sink to his knees, but Gwenyth's arrival, Nan's visits, and his and Gwenyth's subsequent flight had done much to revive his spirits. Anxious sweat trickled down his spine as he scuttled through back alleys.

By Lodar, what he'd give for a bath and clean clothes.

During his first weeks of imprisonment, he'd smelled himself, but he'd become used to the scent. Neither Gwenyth nor Leo had turned up their noses, but he intended to bathe at the first opportunity.

Martinos came to the edge of the buildings. From here, when he glanced back, the castle dominated the skyline. Guard soldiers continued to fly overhead, and apprehension rose in him.

Traversing the open ground without detection provided a challenge. How the devil could he manage this? Never had a hundred feet seemed so far. Once in the forest's coolness, he'd have a better chance of avoiding recapture.

A group of women and children presented an opportunity, and he seized it. He attached himself to the rear of their group and trailed them while attempting to give off timid and harmless vibes.

The children chattered in excitement and skipped alongside their mothers. Increased awareness of his surroundings yanked at him, every sense working overtime. Tension simmered in Martinos's gut, and he had to force himself to amble in a limping gait. A dragon bugled from overhead, and for one horrid second Martinos thought the soldiers had spotted him. His group stopped, forcing him to halt, too, or attract attention. The women and children lifted their heads, holding their hands above their eyes to block the morning sun.

One woman gasped, her wrinkled face holding distaste. "Get away from us, beggar."

"My apologies," Martinos said, bowing his head. *Slouch. Look small. Safe.* "I mean you no harm." But if a dragon spotted him, they'd incinerate the group without a blink.

"How do we know that?" a rail-thin woman snapped, flapping

her arms at him.

"The forest path is best to escape the warmth of the day. I cannot help it if we are walking the same track."

The woman's suspicious pull of lips and furrowed brow didn't shift. "So say you."

"I do say," Martinos said, tired of the conversation and aware of his vulnerable situation. He sidled past the group, keeping his gaze lowered and maintaining hunched shoulders. His beard aged him, but at the first opportunity, he'd ditch the whiskers and find fresh clothes.

Once away from the women and children, he maintained a lumbering pace until he reached the first of the trees. He never looked back. He never increased his speed even though every muscle screamed at him to run.

The women's voices rose in chatter, and a girlish giggle floated after him. Martinos's tension lifted as the group's behavior returned to normal. His luck had turned the moment the guards had shoved Gwenyth into her dungeon cell, but his sister's determination to recapture him would drive the search for him.

He could only guess at what Nan had told his parents, but it was apparent she'd stepped into his shoes once she'd orchestrated the rape charges. Had him imprisoned. Greed had always driven his sister, Nandag, and she'd demanded the best of everything. Clothing. Jewels. Even food. His gut told him jealousy lay at the bottom of this plot.

Envy and greed.

Leonidas, Champion of the Skies, had something Nan needed, which was why she'd agreed to the betrothal and marriage. While the full details of his sister's plot were murky, her motives were transparent, at least to him.

Envy and greed times two.

Martinos trudged along the forest path, and the voices of those behind faded. Leo had instructed him to take the left fork in the road. He hustled as fast as possible despite the lethargy pushing at his limbs and the cut soles of his feet. Capture was not an alternative—not now that luck had wandered into his life. He valued this freedom and everything his parents had given him in the past. Revenge might not be possible, but by Lodar, he'd see his name cleared before he relaxed and became a productive dragon.

He reached another fork in the path. This was the one he required, but the trail meandered into the open again. Leo had warned him of this portion of his journey. Should he wait for dark or risk exposing himself to any dragon flying overhead?

Every instinct screamed for him to travel faster, to escape this place. Martinos paused in the shade of an old tree. He leaned against the tree trunk, the bark rough at his back, and waited, his gaze lifting skyward. In the distance, a range of mountains peeped above the trees. A thunder of dragons flew into sight, operating in what looked like a search pattern.

Idiots. He couldn't fly.

Not long after they'd placed the band on his left biceps, he'd attempted to cut the metal and free his dragon. A blast shock had zapped through him and knocked him out for two days.

He watched the dragons wheel to the right. Were they more interested in finding Leo and recapturing Gwenyth? Martinos spotted a second search party on the horizon. He calculated the risk of running into the open. No, not running. He'd drag himself up and stride through the clearing, keeping an even pace. With a deep breath and one last scan of the sky, Martinos stepped from the shade and hustled toward the human village. Leo's suggestion had been inspired, as long as he could make it to the town without capture.

He understood from the guard's gossip that most dragons on Hissing Isle avoided humans. Leo was an exception—one who enjoyed their company. After meeting Gwenyth and witnessing her mental strength, Martinos appreciated and understood Leo's gravitation toward humans.

Martinos tripped, fatigue stabbing at his limbs, and although the soles of his feet had toughened over the years, tender spots forced him to limp, the pain radiating up his legs. Grit kept him plodding onward and ignoring his assorted injuries.

Early the next day, a hint of briny sea hovered in the air. Apart from the women and children he'd encountered yesterday, he'd seen no one, and his optimism increased.

This plan might work.

If the humans trusted him.

At the last moment, before they'd parted ways, Leo had made a whispered suggestion. Use honesty and tell the humans who he was and what was happening. Tell them Leo had rescued both Martinos and his wife from the dungeon.

He finally reached the outskirts of the village. The human dwellings and businesses hugged a hillside, and a cobblestone road led downward to the sea, where the locals moored their boats. Martinos glanced skyward, scanning for dragons. He spotted several flying over the forest nearer the castle. Martinos kept moving. Two men strode past him, carrying goods on their shoulders. A mother and child emerged from a bakery. Each noticed him but continued with their business. The men nodded while the woman offered a polite smile despite his wooly hair and beard. Martinos limped down the hill to the port. He studied the names of the boats and couldn't find the one he wanted.

Finally, he asked an old mariner who was fixing a fishing net with a long needle and thick thread.

"Excuse me," Martinos said. "Do you know the *Fancy Pete*? Leo told me to ask for Henry."

The elderly man observed him through alert blue eyes. He wore a flat cap over sparse gray hair, and a thick navy jersey lay on the ground to his right. Patches covered his shirt, although the cleanliness was a distinct contrast to Martinos's clothing. Lines carved deep into his tanned face and myriad scars on his hands hinted at a hard-working life.

"Leo, the dragon?" he asked after a measured pause.

"Yes. Leo suggested I ask for Henry. I need passage to Perfume Isle."

"Oh, aye," the man said. "Henry sailed earlier this morning before dawn. He'll be back later today."

Disappointment surged through Martinos, yet he kept his expression neutral. "Is there somewhere I can wait until he returns?"

"Sit with me," the man suggested. "If you're a friend of Leo's, you're a friend to me and the residents of the township. I understand he married a human girl a few days ago. Have you met her?"

Martinos smiled, and the action felt natural. "Gwenyth. She is not only beautiful, but she's kind and smart. I liked her very much."

"Aye, that's what the minister told my Sally. I'm looking forward to meeting her."

Not likely to happen soon, given Nan's determination to see her dead. Gwenyth had been lucky. If it weren't for Nan's decision to make a spectacle of Gwenyth's death, neither he nor Gwenyth would've escaped.

"You'll like her. Leo is a besotted husband, and I mean that in the nicest way. From what I saw, the feeling is mutual."

The man jerked his chin in acknowledgment, his weathered

hands flashing to and fro with the needle as he chatted. "Most of the dragons turn up their noses at us and consider humans inferior. Not Leo. He helps many of us and purchases his supplies here. He's an honorable man. Generous too."

"That he is," Martinos said, meaning every word.

"Once I'm done here, come back to my cottage with me. My Sally will make us a meal."

"I appreciate the offer, but I'd hate to miss Henry. I must get to Perfume Isle."

"Don't fear." The man grinned at him, a sincere gap-toothed smile. "Henry will be around to see Sally and me before he leaves again. He's my son."

A rusty laugh escaped Martinos. "Well, in that case, I'd appreciate a meal. I'm Martinos. I don't suppose you could tell me where to purchase clothes and get my beard trimmed. Bathe?"

The man nodded. "The name is Sam, and I can help with clothes. I have old ones that no longer fit me." He patted his stomach. "We're the same size apart from my belly. You can clean up at my home."

"I have no way of repaying you."

Sam tilted his head as if considering him. "Do you know how to mend a net?"

"No," Martinos said. "But I'm willing to learn."

CHAPTER 3

Escape to Holy Island

The place where Liza's car had gone over the cliff was easy enough to spot. Orange traffic cones blocked one half of the road. A barely out-of-school police constable held a two-way radio in one hand, coordinating with another to direct traffic. Police vehicles and unmarked cars parked farther along the road. Bright yellow warning tape helped to preserve the site.

Cherry swallowed, the officialness of the location bringing reality. Liza had disappeared—not precisely accurate if Rena's tale was true, but that was what she'd decided to embrace—and she and Rena had colluded to kidnap Liza's daughter. If the police caught them, they'd land in a world populated with Tony's smug

I-told-you-so. But Liza had fought Tony for custody. She'd clashed in the court, and the judge had agreed with Liza's argument.

This, however, was different. Cherry never broke laws, and right now, nauseous anxiety tumbled like a gymnast at the pit of her stomach. She was a people pleaser—someone who followed rules.

A friendship with Liza and Rena had taught her she'd crossed to the other side—to door-mat territory. *Heck. Tell the truth.* She'd let her mother boss her around for years. Her single act of rebellion—buying the bookstore and moving into the flat above the premises.

What to do?

She halted behind a tractor and waited for the constable to signal their turn to drive past. Although she'd contacted the police yesterday, she hated to push her luck. They might withhold information from anyone except family.

No, best to continue to Holy Island. Abiding by strong advice, aka rules, she'd checked the website for the day's causeway times. Plenty of time for morning tea at a village. She'd snap photos too if she found a picturesque stop. Since Joanna enjoyed painting so much, she'd brought her an oversize sketchpad along with watercolor paints and crayons. Joanna loved using photos as inspiration to draw in her sketchpad, or they could make an anonymous online photo album to share later.

Activities to keep Joanna busy and engaged while she and Rena planned their next steps.

As if on cue, the phone rang. Cherry eyed the cop whose attention was on the line of oncoming vehicles and risked answering. Even so, guilt assailed her. *Bad girl, Cherry.* "Rena, I can't talk, but I intend to stop at the next village for a cuppa. Can I ring you then?"

"Sure thing," Rena said.

Cherry ended the call and followed the tractor once the constable signaled it was their turn to drive along the one-lane road.

She tried not to glance at the police activity on the beach, but it was impossible to miss the divers with their oxygen tanks. Her eyes stung, and she blinked while wishing there was some way to help search for Liza. Rena couldn't be right. Could she? Her throat ached, and she gasped her next breath. The hoarse sound reverberated through the car interior.

With her eyes on the road and her hands white-knuckling the steering wheel, Cherry sensed Joanna's curiosity. Cherry coughed, forced herself to pull it together for Joanna's sake. Later, when she was alone, she could release her fears, her deep sorrow, her pain at losing her friend. Then, she'd pull herself up by her bootstraps and step up for Joanna. She refused to revert to her old pattern of hiding and pretending everything was marvelous.

"What are they doing?" Joanna studied the divers in wetsuits with curiosity as they backed into the water, carrying oxygen tanks.

"I'm not sure," Cherry lied, and that stupid lump bloomed

again in her throat. "Aunt Rena wants me to call. I thought we'd stop for a cup of tea. Are you hungry?"

"I could eat," Joanna said, her offhand manner making Cherry smile.

"I don't know where you put the food you eat," Cherry said. "You must have hollow legs."

"Have I?" Joanna cocked her head, reminding Cherry of an inquisitive bird. "Daddy's girlfriend told him I have worms."

Cherry gaped at Joanna before returning her gaze to the road. The tractor turned into a field, and she accelerated past. "You don't have worms."

Joanna frowned. "Daddy's girlfriend said I'd get an itchy bottom and—"

"Your father's girlfriend is mistaken. There is nothing wrong with your appetite. When you're young, you should try lots of fresh foods. It's the time when you decide what vegetables and fruit you enjoy eating. If she says that again, you tell her you're experimenting and refining your palate. Can you remember that?"

"Yes." Joanna lifted her nose, her mouth pursing. "I'm six now. I remember lots of stuff."

"Outstanding job," Cherry said, suppressing a smile and concealing a pang of pain. She'd seen Liza make that same expression. "See that island way over there? The one with the buildings?"

"Yes."

"That is where we're going for a vacation."

"When will Mummy come?"

"As s-soon as she's finished her dragon research," Cherry said, the lie tasting foul on her tongue. But she and Rena had agreed they'd keep the truth from Joanna until Liza's whereabouts were confirmed.

As they reached the village outskirts, Cherry slowed to the reduced speed limit. "Keep an eye out for a teashop."

"I see a picture of a teapot," Joanna shouted a few minutes later.

"Excellent. We need to find parking—ah! We'll follow these signs to get to the parking lot."

Soon, Cherry and Joanna wandered back to the teashop. It was a delightful old building with whitewashed walls and a black timber skeleton dividing the white sections. Inside, several tables held customers, and an enticing cheese-scone scent wafted on the air to greet them.

"They do cream teas. How about a scone with jam and clotted cream?"

"Yes, please!" Joanna exclaimed. Her enthusiasm dimmed a fraction. "I promise not to spill jam on my clothes."

At the counter, a teenage girl with bright red hair and freckles took their order. Cherry handed over a twenty-pound note. "When did you get jam on your clothes?"

"When Daddy and I went out with his girlfriend. She got mad because I dropped jam on my dress and her dress too. I didn't mean to let it drip off my knife."

"No one spills food on purpose," Cherry said, mentally castigating the woman for her preciousness. "Don't worry. If your clothes get dirty, we'll throw them into the washing machine. No problem."

Joanna grinned and nodded hard enough to make her scrunchie-covered bun bounce.

"Let's sit over there by the window so we can people watch," Cherry suggested.

"What is people watching?"

Cherry tweaked Joanna's nose. The kid was so cute. One of Cherry's regrets. She'd love to have children, but a man was necessary for that dream to mature. "If we watch the men and women and children who walk past the teashop, we call that people watching. When I was your age, I'd imagine where they were going or what they did for a job."

"I'll play," Joanna said. "If I remember them, I can draw them later."

"You watch the next three people walking past while I call Aunt Rena. After I hang up, you can describe them to me. Tell me where they're going. Okay?"

Joanna cocked her head as an older man *tap-tap-tapped* his way along the sidewalk.

Cherry dialed Rena. "Have you heard anything?"

"They found Liza's car," Rena said through a tear-thickened

voice. "The divers searched for Liza but didn't find a body. They said someone severed the seatbelt."

Cherry swallowed hard and glanced at Joanna. Liza's daughter was still peering out the window at the village locals and visitors. "What happens next?"

"The divers are continuing their search, but the water is murkier than usual. They only spotted the c-car because it's bright red."

"What will we do?"

"Continue to Holy Island and lie low there, I guess. Robe Guy told me we should go to Lindisfarne."

"But it was a dream. He's not real."

"Do you have a better idea? Besides, the causeway restricts travel for part of the day. Tony won't find us. Not easily."

"Are you coming to meet us?"

"I've decided I'll contact Dad after all. Call him in Los Angeles and ask him what he thinks we should do," Rena said.

"Talk to you soon." Cherry forced out the words, the urge to cry strong. She hated to scare Joanna, so she sucked up her pain and swallowed hard to shift the stubborn lump blocking her throat. Rena's story about Liza being alive was just that—a fabrication. She struggled for composure.

"D-describe the people you've seen," she said to Joanna. "What is their story?"

She and Joanna demolished their scones, drank tea, and discussed the passersby. Soon, an hour had passed. It was time to leave if they wanted to reach the causeway for the crossing. Although Cherry hadn't visited Holy Island before, she'd read of the dangers. Each year visitors lost vehicles to the sea because of the rapidly incoming tide. The rescue services had to save the hapless passengers. Racing the speedy water was the height of idiocy.

When they reached the crossing, half a dozen vehicles waited for the road to open. Some were tourists while others were locals who'd topped up on supplies.

Cherry had booked accommodation in a cottage. She'd intended to book a bed-and-breakfast before deciding the owners might pose nosy questions. It was better to rent a self-catering cottage and keep to themselves as much as possible. When Rena joined them, she could have her own room.

"Does the sea cover the road? It's wet," Joanna said as they proceeded in convoy.

"Yes, when the tide comes in each day. That's why we needed to wait at the teashop."

"Oh," Joanna said, her eyes wide with interest.

The sea splashed the sides of the road, and the surface bore wet patches. The possibility of calamity made the drive spooky, and her hands shook before she tightened them on the steering wheel. A mile had never seemed so long, but soon Cherry drove onto the island proper. A bus trailed them, plus a smaller minivan. The number of tourists surprised Cherry. From the research she'd done, she knew the island hosted lots of day-trippers. Would she and Joanna stand out? She needed a solid story—one close to the truth for her to remember the details, yet nothing to raise suspicions in curious locals.

"Our cottage should be easy to find. It's near the beach so we can go for walks." The cottage's isolation worked well, yet it was within walking distance of the island village.

Rena rang again just as they pulled up at the farmhouse where she needed to pick up the keys for the cottage.

"Rena, I'll call back in ten minutes," Cherry said without letting her friend speak.

"Where is my daughter?" A masculine voice growled.

Cherry hung up, her heart knocking against her ribs. She powered off her phone while sending a small prayer of thanks that she'd turned off the location thingie before she'd left home. That's what they did in the page-turner novels she read to give recommendations to her thriller customers.

Stupid! She should've checked the screen before she answered. Cherry scowled at her phone and set it in the console.

"Sweetie, wait here for me while I grab the keys to our cottage."

"Will I be able to see the sea?"

"I'm not sure," Cherry said. "We'll have our answer as soon as we arrive."

"Can I pick my bedroom?"

Cherry touched the tip of Joanna's nose. The girl reminded Cherry of Liza, and pain sliced through her confidence. She curled her nails into her palms and forced herself to stride to the door and knock. Were she and Rena doing the right thing? Withholding the truth from Joanna felt like a betrayal. Tears filled her eyes, and she wiped them away with an impatient stroke of her hand. She'd turned into a watering can, and crying didn't help one bit.

"Hello." An elderly woman with a rotund figure sent her a polite smile. A dusting of flour covered one of her rosy cheeks while wisps of her steel-gray hair had escaped her ponytail. "Can I help you?"

"I'm Cherry Lawford. I spoke to you on the phone about renting your cottage for two weeks."

"Most people come for a few days. It's not a big island," the woman commented.

"I've been ill," Cherry said. Her pale, red-eyed reflection in the mirror this morning made this a realistic excuse. "I need somewhere quiet to rest. I'm from London, and my friends mentioned the island. Believe me, I'm looking forward to beach walks and the simpler pleasures." She laughed. "I used to love baking. Maybe I'll get back to making bread."

The woman nodded. "I wanted to temper your expectations if you're expecting a busy nightlife on Holy Island."

"I noticed you have a pub. Dinner and a drink at the pub is enough excitement for me."

"I'll get the keys. You realize you won't find a supermarket here?"

"Yes, I read the small print on your website regarding the island services. I'm prepared. My niece and I won't host noisy parties or break any of your rules. We're looking forward to visiting the island sites."

The woman disappeared and reappeared with the rattle of keys. Cherry straightened from her slouch and pinned a smile in place. A friendly and sincere one, she hoped. A non-troublemaking one. A smile that said move along—nothing to see here. No kidnapping of children or stepping outside the bounds of the law. *No, not me.*

The woman handed over a bunch of keys. "Drive along this road, take the first left, and you'll see the cottage on its own. Use the garage if you want. You'll find my number by the phone in the cottage. Call if you need help."

"Thanks," Cherry said.

She returned to her car and waved farewell with a cheerfulness she forced. Minutes later, she pulled up on the cobblestones outside a red garage. "This is it, Joanna. What do you think?"

"It looks like a storybook house."

And it did. The cottage was an old farm building, and the brick exterior displayed a charming aging. Ivy clung to one corner and shutters guarded the windows. The photos she'd seen online had shown a modern interior with views of the castle and the sea. To the rear of the cottage, a private garden provided a temptation to explore outside. Two mature trees, one with a swing that'd entice Joanna, offered shade while a green hedge provided privacy from ramblers. A white gate allowed access to the beach. Nearer the deck, the garden beds held a collection of flowers in red, yellow, purple, and white. The perfect spot to eat outdoor meals if the weather remained warm.

Cherry climbed out of the car and grabbed several of their bags.

Although there were eateries in the village, she'd brought enough food for three days. They'd keep away from the town during the busy visitor time when the causeway was accessible. If they decided on a meal out, it'd be when the tourists left and the island numbers returned to the regular two hundred residents. Once the food ran low, she'd replenish in Bamburgh on the mainland where she and Joanna would remain anonymous amongst the larger number of residents and tourists.

Joanna ran past her, carrying her doll and her bag containing art supplies. "I get to choose my room."

Cherry set her bag in the main bedroom before leaving Joanna to choose her favorite.

"This one," Joanna said.

It was the smallest bedroom with a single bed and access to the deck. Joanna stood at the window and let out a loud sigh, once again sounding so much like her mother, Cherry had to bite back another wave of tears.

"I can see the sea. Perfect," Joanna said.

"Help me unload the rest of our things and put away the food, then we can go for a walk. Can you unpack and put away your things for me?"

Five minutes later, they headed outside for the beach. Cherry dithered over her phone and decided she'd better turn it back on—just in case. She checked the number Tony had called from and gasped when she noted it was Rena's. If he'd hurt Rena, she'd go attack-woman on his butt. The man was a bully.

She noted she'd received several texts from a number she didn't recognize. She read them, and the tension in her shoulders eased. The messages were from Rena.

Cherry dialed the number Rena told her to call. "Rena, it's Cherry. What happened? Why does Tony have your phone?"

"The bastard jumped me. He was waiting when I left my house and forced me back inside before I knew what was happening. He locked me in the bathroom, and it took me ages to wriggle through the window."

"Are you okay?"

"I have bruises, and I complained to the police."

Cherry gasped. "Did they ask about Joanna?"

"I explained the position to the police and the reasons Tony wants his daughter. I showed them the court documents. After talking to Dad, I took his lawyer with me. At this stage, the police will leave Joanna in our care, due to the circumstances, so you won't have to worry the police will knock on your door."

"Are you pressing charges against Tony?"

"Damn straight," Rena snapped. "The lawyer suggested I give the cops a statement. I'm still coming to the island, but it will be a few days before I arrive. I need to dodge the bloody man. The toad is staking out my house."

"Be careful. Liza mentioned he has a temper. He's likely to hurt you to get his way."

"Let him try again," Rena snapped. "He took me by surprise. He won't a second time."

CHAPTER 4

Dragon Overboard

Martinos stood on the wooden jetty with Sam as Henry and his crew sailed into port.

"Times are difficult, and fish are hard to find," Sam said. "This catch looks small. My bet—he'll want to go out again early in the morning."

"Won't your son be exhausted?" Martinos asked.

Sam shrugged. "He has a young family and needs the money."

Martinos nodded and wished he could pay Henry for his passage. Perhaps he should've asked Leo for a loan before he came. He doubted he'd have many possessions left on Smoking Isle after Nan carried out her skullduggery. "Will he accept my help to unload?"

"I'm sure he will," Sam said. "Come along, and I'll introduce you."

Martinos followed Sam to where Henry had nosed his fishing boat into the jetty.

The wooden vessel wasn't large, although it appeared sturdy and in excellent repair. Three men stood on board, one behind the wheel, while the other two held ropes ready to tie the vessel to its mooring spot.

"Henry, this is Martinos," Sam said once the crew had berthed. "Leo sent him in our direction. Martinos seeks passage to Perfume Isle."

"Or Smoking Isle, if you're traveling that far. I don't have money to give you at the moment, but I promise to pay you in the future. Meantime, I can work for my passage."

"Why should I trust you?" Henry demanded. Shadows darkened the area beneath his reddened eyes, and his shoulders hunched in a worn-down attitude.

Martinos shrugged and attempted to maintain a serene expression without giving away his inner turmoil. Henry was his one chance of leaving Hissing Isle. If Henry refused to take him, he wasn't sure what he'd do.

"You're a dragon," Henry said. "It's easy to tell by your height and breadth. Why don't you fly?"

"I can't fly," Martinos said with a shrug. "My fellow dragons consider me useless, which is why I'm asking you to take me. The moment I get my hands on money, I will bring you a payment, and meantime, I can help."

"Do you know how to sail a boat?"

Martinos nodded. "I sailed as a youngster. I'm not a stranger to the water or boats."

Henry nodded. "I'd appreciate a hand unloading the catch."

"Consider it done." Martinos stepped closer. While he acted with confidence, he prayed he didn't fall flat on his face. After being behind bars for three years and his frantic rush through the forest, every bone and muscle in his body throbbed. His feet were a mess of cuts and tender spots, and he had to concentrate on halting his instinct to limp. Still, he was so close to freedom, he could taste it.

"Once I unload, I'm off home for dinner and to see my wife. High tide is at six in the morning. We'll head off then."

Martinos helped Henry carry a load of fish off the boat and stack it on a trolley. The two crew members wheeled the cart away, their faces lined with the same fatigue etched into their skipper. With the unloading complete, Henry trudged off, leaving Martinos staring after him.

"Do you have somewhere to stay?" Sam asked.

Martinos shook his head.

"We have a spare room. You're welcome to stay with us."

"Thank you so much," Martinos said. "I will repay you when I can." Martinos met Sam's gaze and held it. "You have my oath."

"If you're Leo's friend, you'll find most of us will go the extra mile for you."

Martinos nodded because emotion grabbed him by the throat and blocked his words. Leo hadn't trusted him—not entirely—but because of Gwenyth, he'd offered Martinos a lifeline. During his trip through the forest, he'd promised himself he'd repay Leo and Gwenyth for their kindness. He hoped the pair had escaped his sister and the castle soldiers because Nan's fury lashed anyone who stood in the way. His sister wouldn't hesitate to kill Gwenyth once she got her hands on the usurper who'd ruined her grandiose plans.

At six the next morning, Martinos waited at the wharf for Henry and his crew. Sam had sent him off with food and good wishes, and Martinos made another silent vow to repay Henry and Sam for helping him. It was obvious they scraped by, and Martinos promised himself he'd reward them for their generosity.

Considering dragons' arrogance and lack of charity, Martinos was grateful these human men hadn't rebuffed him in retaliation for other's actions.

"My fishing skills are rusty," Martinos told Henry. "But I can take instructions and will do my best to do as you ask. All you need to do is tell me."

"You're like Leo," Henry observed, his brown eyes narrowed against the rising sun. The sleep had helped his bloodshot eyes.

"He treats us as equals and has helped many a local family who was desperate for aid. The women sighed in sorrow when we learned he'd married."

"Leo is a lucky man. Gwenyth has heart and courage," Martinos said, sincere in his compliment. "She is captivating, and it's easy to understand why Leo fell for her."

"The minister and his wife told everyone who asked that she was worthy of Leo. Is she truly a human?"

"She is." Martinos hesitated, then went with the truth as Leo had suggested. "After Leo and Gwenyth left here, they flew to the castle. Leo's parents had arranged a betrothal for him with another dragon. Once they learned of Leo's marriage, they seized Gwenyth and placed her in the castle dungeon."

Henry turned to Martinos, his mouth slackening. He started to speak, stopped, then tried again. "Is she all right? What did Leo do?"

"From what I understand, they zapped Leo and seized Gwenyth while he was unconscious. Leo dug into the dungeon to rescue his wife. They escaped and have flown to Perfume Isle to take refuge with Leo's friends."

Henry's fists clenched at his sides. "I loathe the way the dragons treat humans."

"They mistreat their own race—those they consider inferior dragons," Martinos said.

The crew lifted a sail, and Henry maneuvered his boat past the breakwater and into open sea before he replied. "I hadn't heard that."

"It's true. It's the reason I can't fly. I irritated the wrong people and received a punishment in return. They suppressed my dragon." The waves were more prominent now, and Martinos grasped a wooden ledge to keep his balance.

"Those clouds are iffy," Henry said as he scanned the sky. "I'd stay ashore, but I need the funds. Do you get seasick?"

"No, I'm fine," Martinos said.

Henry jerked his head at the two crewmates. "Harry over there has a weak stomach. He'll start puking soon."

"How far out are you going?"

"I have several favorite spots, depending on the weather. Today, we'll head for Perfume Isle and fish in the shelter of one of their bays."

Harry made a run for the boat railing and vomited over the side. The other man—his friend—roared with laughter, finding Harry's weakness a joke.

The waves grew bigger, and the wind whipped Martinos's hair. He was thankful Sam had given him warm clothes since the bracing wind ripped across the water. Sam's wife had pressed food on him this morning. Yes, he had much to be thankful for this stormy day.

"Change of plans," Henry shouted over the wind. "The sea is calmer over to the right. I'll steer the boat in that direction. Much easier than trying to sail to Perfume Isle in a straight line."

Henry wasn't wrong. The waves had grown steadily larger with many towering over their vessel. Their boat bobbed like a stick, which ill-suited Harry. The crewman slumped against the boat's side in abject misery between waves. Now and then, he'd stand on wobbly legs to vomit yet again. His friend had ceased his laughter and gripped the opening leading below deck, his expression grim.

Without warning, the sail whipped loose.

"Take the wheel," Henry hollered, gesturing at Martinos. "Giles and I will fix the sail."

"Which way do you want me to steer?"

"Aim toward the flatter bit of water," Henry shouted. Once Martinos had control of the wheel, he crab-walked over to where Giles and Harry struggled to gather the sail. The canvas snapped in a fury, eluding the men's grasping hands. Martinos watched for an instant before he focused on the task Henry had set him.

It took every ounce of strength to hold the vessel steady. The boat made slow progress, drifting and heading with the wind instead of the direction Henry wanted. Martinos white-knuckled the wheel and struggled to hold the course. The wind wailed and ranted. Waves towered overhead, constantly splashing the deck and soaking everyone and thing on it.

Martinos kept fighting, his muscles straining as he battled nature. A tap on his shoulder had him jumping in alarm.

"Superb job," Henry shouted. "I'll take the wheel."

Martinos nodded but didn't move until Henry regained command of his boat. He stepped back, his gaze on the sea. The calm water was still ahead and to their right.

"Does the sea always have strange patches like this?" he asked.

Henry's frown was clear. "This is unusual. I've never seen the like. *Hell.*" His eyes widened in panic, and Martinos spun to check on the source of his alarm.

A low croak escaped Martinos. Horror lifted the hair at his nape, terror rooting him to the spot.

An immense wave approached the left side of their vessel, towering over them.

A rogue wave.

Seconds later, water rushed the deck, a mighty churn of white foam. Martinos grabbed for purchase too late. The wall of seawater swept him overboard. The last thing he saw before the sea closed over his head was Henry's pale shock.

Martinos fought to the surface, gasping for breath. Another wave slammed him, sending him under. The water shoved him, threw him down, and tossed him skyward. For a second, he glimpsed land before yet another wave broke, engulfing him and obscuring his vision. He kicked and swam underwater until the press on his lungs had him desperate for air. When he came up again, the waves were smaller. He scanned the sea for the boat. It wasn't within sight. He trod water and did a three-sixty: only sea and the slice of sand to his right, otherwise the sea was empty of fishing vessels.

Martinos struggled toward shore, bobbing under the surface several times, fighting with the power of the waves and struggling to keep afloat. His breaths seesawed—sharp rasps edged with alarm. Every second breath contained water, and his apprehension ratcheted upward.

No matter how hard he strained, the beach didn't get any closer. He was tiring now, finding swimming difficult. He gasped. Spluttered. Bobbed, powerless against the current and the ferocious waves. Then, a miracle. His foot touched the bottom, and he dragged himself closer to the shore.

He blinked blearily and spewed out water. He had trouble concentrating, but he fought from the sea, tussling his urge to give up. Finally, finally, he reached clear sand and toppled like a tree. He struck the ground, full of gratitude that he'd reached the shore.

After a long moment, he dragged his body higher onto the sand. He pushed himself upright and searched for Henry's boat. The air shimmered, and he blinked to focus. His view continued to glow, and the calm sea shocked him rigid. That couldn't be right. Where were the gigantic waves that only minutes earlier threatened to end his life? Martinos squinted, and the sea remained calm, the scene wavering and reflecting to him in weird images. Then everything snapped into place, and gentle waves whooshed to shore. He shook his head, disorientated.

The events here were not ordinary.

He pushed himself to his knees and attempted to stand. For a moment, he thought he'd manage, but his legs held the strength of a twig. He wavered for several steps before he fell.

His stomach roiled, and his back curved as he vomited up more seawater.

"Are you all right?"

The feminine voice had him stiffening, but no. It wasn't his imagination. Two feet stood in front of him. No four. He strained to raise his head and gaped at the woman with red hair and creamy skin who was staring down at him. Beside her stood a child who brought to mind Gwenyth.

"Where am I?" he croaked.

"You're on Lindisfarne." When he stared at her, she said. "Holy Island."

Her voice was melodic and sweet, and her worry for her safety and that of the child became evident when she retreated half a step, tugging the girl with her.

"I mean you no harm," he whispered. "I'm confused. An enormous wave swept me off the boat. We were headed to Perfume Isle."

"Perfume Isle?" Her brown eyes studied his face, dissected him and his words. "I've never heard of the place."

CHAPTER 5

He Thinks He's a Dragon

C herry recalled Rena's dream as she stared at the half-drowned man sprawled on the beach. He had tangled black curls, his hair longer than a person in business might wear, while his whisky-brown eyes held secrets. A black beard covered his lower face, and she found herself imagining what he might look like without it. Even though her head warned caution, he intrigued her, and curiosity had her wanting to learn more.

She hadn't believed Rena, but here was living proof. Cherry continued to gawk at the man, hesitating over what to do next. Did she offer her help or walk away without a backward glance?

The man's attention drifted to Joanna, and his eyes widened as if he recognized her.

Cherry's suspicions sped in a different direction. Surely Tony hadn't caught up to them already? No, that wasn't possible. She and Rena had been careful and made sure Cherry's leaving had coincided with the school drop-off time.

"What is your name?" Cherry asked. "Where are you from?"

"My home is on Smoking Isle," he said without hesitation. "Although I haven't lived there for a long time."

"Why not?" Cherry took another half-step backward and dragged Joanna with her. Liza's daughter had remained silent to this point, but Cherry suspected the child's questions might burst free soon. Joanna held a powerful yearning to learn things—even subjects that drifted into gossip territory. Liza tried to teach her daughter right from wrong with rumors and hearsay, but it was a slow and frustrating process. Tony didn't help.

"My name is Martinos," he said, ignoring her question regarding his home.

The stranger had a faint accent. Since she lived in England, she was used to regional and foreign accents. On any one day, she might hear residents from Devon, from Manchester or Liverpool. Sometimes, her customers sounded more exotic with Antipodean, South African, or an occasional American visitor to her store. She had an excellent ear and made it a game to guess their country of origin. Martinos's enunciation and his name were unusual.

"I've never heard of Smoking Isle. Where is it?"

A frown creased his forehead, and he hesitated. "Not far from here."

"Now I know you're lying. The Faro Islands are close, but they're the only islands in the vicinity," Cherry snapped. "If you're positive you don't require medical assistance, we'll leave you to your rest. Come, Joanna."

Instead of accepting her brushoff, Martinos grew more alert. "Your daughter, she reminds me of a woman I met a few days ago. Do you know a human called Gwenyth?"

Cherry stared, realized her mouth had dropped open in a full-out gape, and snapped her teeth together. "Human?" she asked instead of questioning him further.

Martinos frowned again, the action not dimming his attractiveness. With his long legs, she assumed he was taller than her. His broad shoulders strained the seams of his shirt, but his pale skin indicated he might've been sick. He was a difficult man to read.

Her warning signals should be blaring.

Empty beach. Strange man. *Danger.*

Yet each time his gaze drifted to Joanna, and it was often, the angles of his face softened, and a tiny smile played around his sensual lips as if pleasant thoughts filled his mind or he'd recalled a treasured memory. Then there was the fact Rena had told her she'd meet a man on the beach.

"Are you going to answer me?" Cherry demanded.

His gaze darted from Joanna to her. His frown deepened a
fraction more before it eased. "Yes," he said. "But please humor me
and answer one question first?"

"If I can," Cherry said.

"Are we on the mainland?"

"No, I told you. We're on Holy Island as the locals call it. You
can see the mainland over there." Cherry gestured at the landmass
on the horizon, visible on this cloudless day.

"Why is the island called Holy Island?"

Cherry flashed a grin without meaning to, and Martinos smiled
in return. It took his face from interesting to arresting. "The
island played an important part in bringing the Christian gospel to
England. A young monk called Aidan established an abbey here.
It's in ruins now, but Joanna and I intend to visit while we're here."

Martinos's eyes widened. "Druids?"

"No, monks. Why did you say human?" she asked, weirded out
by the way he'd called this Gwenyth woman a human. Weren't
they all humans? His voice *had* softened when he mentioned the
woman, so it hadn't been a derogatory term.

"I'm hungry," Joanna said.

"You are so alike," Martinos whispered. "You could be mother
and daughter."

His words had Cherry snapping to attention. Was it possible?
She sucked in a breath between her teeth, the hiss jerking
Martinos's attention back to her. Rena's dream man had claimed

Liza was still alive.

"I said human because where I come from, two different species occupy the island. Humans and dragon shifters."

Cherry wilted, her optimism bleeding from her like the air from a punctured balloon. What a pity. He'd hit his head and was now spouting utter rubbish. She'd humor him. Let him dig a deeper hole. "And you are?"

"A dragon," he said.

"Mummy likes dragons," Joanna shared. "She writes stories."

"Joanna, why don't you walk that way and search for colorful shells or stones or tiny pieces of driftwood? Remember, I promised to show you how to make a beach collage, so you can do one and hold your own art show here."

"Okay, Aunt Cherry," Joanna trilled.

"Stay in sight. That means if you can't see me, then you've gone too far, and you must come straight back."

"That's what Mummy says," she said with a mischievous grin.

"I know. Off you go. I'll watch you," Cherry said.

Joanna skipped along the waterline, her attention on the sand.

Once Joanna was out of earshot, she shifted to see both Martinos and Joanna. "If you're a dragon, prove it. Shift to your other form. The beach is empty, and there's only me and Joanna who will witness your shift."

"I can't."

"Because you're lying. Dragons are storybook creatures."

Martinos tapped the broad copper-colored band on his left biceps. "This armband keeps my dragon contained. We no longer communicate. It's like part of me has died," he said in a bleak voice. "My tattoo shows a sleeping dragon. See?"

He unbuttoned his shirt and parted the front before she gathered her wits to tell him to stop. She glimpsed a broad, hairless chest. Low on his belly, a red tattooed figure curled in a tight ball. It was difficult to see. Perhaps a dog? She cocked her head. Perhaps a dragon if she employed her imagination.

She lifted her gaze to meet his and ignored the punch of heat that struck her chest and sank downward. "How come humans live with dragons?"

He hesitated before answering. "Years ago, before the last dragon died on the mainland, we mixed freely with humans. Most humans didn't understand this and were clueless. We trusted a few friends with the truth. But whenever we were in our dragon form, some humans turned stupid. They didn't understand or believe we had perfect control. Knights wanting honors killed us. Have you heard of St. George? The knight was worse than most.

"Our people held a meeting with the heads of our families in attendance. We retreated to the Dragon Isles and paid the druids to design a spell to hide them from human eyes. The druids charge our clans an annual tithe to maintain the barrier. As long as we pay, our lands are undetected by those on the mainland."

"And the humans where you live?"

"At the time when the druids cast their spell, our islands were a haven. Several boatloads of Viking warriors had wrecked on the rocky shores and made their home there. Smugglers and a few humans running from the law also lived on the islands. We allowed them to stay. Their descendants remain to this day."

"Why are you telling me this?" Cherry asked. At first, despite Rena's assertions, she'd thought he was looney-tunes, yet conviction rang in his voice. Truth. If his tale was a load of lies, he was a gifted storyteller. He hadn't faltered. Not once.

"Because you asked me where I'd been when I wasn't at home. For the last three years, I've been in the dungeon at Castle Caireall."

Cherry tensed, poised to flee. "Why?"

"It's a long story, but the charges were rape, which ended in the girl killing herself."

Cherry gasped and backed up, her apprehension kicking up several notches higher. She glanced at Joanna to ensure she was safe.

"I didn't do it. I did not rape that girl."

"Guilty men and women say that all the time." Cherry eyed him closely as she spoke. Rena had told her to trust this man, to help him. At the time, she'd scoffed, but now she'd met him, and he needed aid. But a dragon? Really.

"I can't make you believe me." He struggled to his feet as a wave thundered to shore in a flurry of power and white foam.

Cherry let out a squeak of alarm and darted back.

"Please. Don't run. On my oath, I did not hurt that girl. Gwenyth trusted me, and she talked Leo into taking me with them when we broke out of the dungeon."

"This Gwenyth was in jail?" She ceased her retreat but remained watchful.

"In the dungeon. Yes. She married Leonidas, Champion of the Skies, and that upset my sister Nandag, The Strongminded." He shook his head. "Nandag wishes to marry Leonidas, and she was intent on getting rid of Gwenyth. She talked like you. Gwenyth, not my sister."

"Describe her to me."

"She had long brown hair and brown eyes. She is around your height—no, a bit taller. Slender. She recently married Leo. I got the impression it was a hurried affair to stop my sister, but Leo is protective of Gwenyth. His jealousy and mistrust of me were clear, but Gwenyth wasn't interested in me in that way. She lit up when Leo came to her rescue."

Cherry tried not to leap to conclusions, despite Rena's earlier assertion. Doppelgangers were more common than one imagined. The way Martinos had stared at Joanna—as if he genuinely recognized her. Not with lust or sick longing, but more reverence with a tinge of amusement and Cherry wanted to say friendship.

"Joanna's mother, Liza, disappeared a few days ago. The police discovered her car submerged in the sea but didn't find her body. They're still searching but have found no sign of her."

"There's something wrong with the barrier," Martinos murmured. "Are you wondering if Gwenyth is your friend?"

Cherry opened and closed her mouth a few times. She wanted to believe this—more than anything. A sigh whooshed free. Such a huge leap. "I don't know what I'm saying. I mean, you can't prove you're a dragon. Liza's disappearance has rattled me." She blinked hard as distress speared her. "I-I pray Liza is alive, so I don't have to tell Joanna her mother is gone. Liza and Joanna have been through so much."

"The local druid representative could help prove my story."

"Sure, I'll do an internet search and locate one straight away," Cherry said with a hint of sarcasm.

"You can do that? Why didn't you say? Where do I find this internet?"

"Popsicles!" she muttered, reverting to the word she, Rena, and Liza had settled on when they wished to swear without giving Joanna superfluous words for her vocabulary. If Martinos was putting on an act, he wasn't slipping. Not one bit. Her mind drifted to Rena, and she sighed, knowing she was going to take a leap and trust her friend's instructions and this stranger. "What do you expect the druid to do?"

"First, I'd ask him to remove the spell on my armband and free my dragon. No doubt, his fee will be exorbitant. He won't do the reversal spell for nothing." Martinos scowled. "I won't know until I ask. Second, I need to investigate the break in the barrier.

I shouldn't have crossed this way. If Gwenyth *is* your friend, she shouldn't have traveled through the barrier to Dragon Isles either. There is something wrong—"

He broke off without warning, his expression turning thoughtful. "I wonder if my sister has something to do with this."

"You mean someone is breaking the barrier that separates your world from mine on purpose?" Cherry asked, more intrigued than she cared to admit. "Why? Is there trouble in your world?"

Martinos thought back to everything he'd learned from the guards' conversations, from the things Leo and Gwenyth had mentioned, from Nan's boldness and her audacity in visiting him to gloat. Things weren't perfect in the Dragon Isles.

An undercurrent of unsavory was creeping into prominence. For example, the growing tension between dragons and humans. The despicable way his people treated those who lived in the human village. The humans worked hard for little compensation. Henry had risked going out in stormy weather because he required the money to pay his men and support his family and his aging parents. Leo was one of the few who championed humans and purchased their goods.

If—*when*—Martinos found his way back to Smoking Isle, he'd bet he'd find the human village on his home island was in similar straits, if not worse, since Nan had been in charge.

He nodded. "I've been out of contact since my imprisonment,

but the things I saw after my escape make me suspect problems. Before, I was too arrogant to see."

"Why would someone break the barrier? It'd place everyone in danger."

"I have no answers. I—you didn't tell me your name," he said, although he'd heard the child call her Aunt Cherry.

"Cherry Lawford," she said after a brief hesitation. A wash of pink invaded her creamy cheeks. She wasn't as tall as Gwenyth and bore a rounded shape his sister and her friends might—no—*would* insult. To his eyes, Cherry possessed delightful curves that enticed his fingers to touch. She wore an indigo blue pair of trews that clung to her backside while her breasts pushed at a form-fitting masculine-styled shirt. This, too, was constructed from a fabric he hadn't seen before. Her lack of trust galled him, although part of him understood. He was a strange man on an isolated beach, and she was responsible for a child.

He was an unknown.

But he had to charm her into offering him aid. He had no other contacts in this world, and he couldn't go forth and pour his outlandish tale into everyone's ears. Cherry was his sole option, his one chance to fit in with her world.

He lifted his head and summoned the energy to push to his feet. A moan escaped, and pain sang along his right side. His feet, too, protested his weight. A nasty scrape on his ribs throbbed.

"How did you injure yourself?"

"I was on a boat traveling between Hissing and Perfume Isles. It must've happened when the wave washed me overboard."

"You need medical attention."

He nodded, and for the millionth time, he wished he and his dragon could communicate—not merely for companionship but because dragons aided their other halves in healing.

"You can come back to my cottage. I'll check your side, and you can eat with us. If you step a foot out of line, I have my phone. I'll call the cops."

Martinos inclined his head. "You don't know me, and you're right to withhold your trust. But I promise you now. I will never hurt you, and if Joanna is related to Gwenyth, I will protect the child with my life. If it weren't for Gwenyth interceding with her mate, I'd still be in the dungeon. My words are empty until I back them up with actions. I understand that and vow to give you solid deeds to help you trust me."

"Even if you hadn't told me you were a dragon shifter, you would've raised my suspicions with your words. The men I've known speak in pretty lies."

"No untruths from me. I've had plenty of time to think during my captivity. Before my confinement, I was a stupid, spoiled scoundrel. I hope I've changed for the better."

"We've walked a fair distance," Cherry said. "Can you manage? Joanna is an active child, and we've learned to give her plenty of exercise. It means she sleeps better. Joanna!" she called.

The girl lifted her head and waved before picking up one last treasure and popping it into her bucket. She ran toward them in a long curve and arrived in a rush of breathless laughter. "Is it lunchtime yet?"

"It is," Cherry said. "Martinos is coming with us."

"Yay!" Joanna said.

Before Martinos could blink, the child grabbed one of his hands and tugged until he started walking. A surge of protectiveness rushed through him at the child's implicit trust. No one apart from Gwenyth had held such faith in him. He thought back. No, that wasn't true. Sam and his son Henry had placed their trust in him because of Leo's recommendation.

He refused to fail them. Somehow, he'd repay their kindness. He wasn't sure how, but he would not fall short on this mission. It was a stark reminder he had indeed changed from the spoiled and pampered son to a man who grew from his experiences. He'd avoid a lapse to his privileged station.

By the time they reached the sand's edge where the beach gave way to grass, Martinos's breaths emerged in harsh gasps. His slog through the forest yesterday, followed by a fitful night of sleep, had depleted what reserves he'd retained. His dunking in the sea hadn't helped.

"Let me offer aid," Cherry said in an inaudible voice.

Before he could protest, she slipped her arm around his waist.

"The cottage isn't much farther."

"Thanks." Martinos focused on staying upright, but by the time a building came into view, he was leaning heavily on Cherry.

"Joanna, run ahead and open the gate for us."

"Yes, Aunt Cherry."

The child bounced away, still full of irrepressible energy, and envy pushed through Martinos. He laughed at himself. He needed time to recover. A better diet and uninterrupted sleep. He'd get there, but it'd take time. At least here, he was safe from Nan.

He trudged past the white gate under his own steam. Once through, Cherry curled her arm around his waist again and guided him across the grass to the stone cottage. Colorful flowers in yellow, orange, and white filled the garden bed to his right while several mature trees provided shade.

"This way," Cherry said, urging him toward a set of three steps. "Sit here and rest. I'll bring you a drink and something to eat. You can have a shower and rest once I've doctored your wounds. Sit," she repeated before retreating indoors.

Joanna tugged on his shirt. It had dried during the walk to the cottage, and now the salt itched his skin. Martinos smiled at her. "Did you want something?"

"Mr. Martin, where will you sleep? Will you sleep in Aunt Cherry's bed? My daddy's girlfriend sleeps in his bed."

A choking sound had him turning his head toward the doorway. Cherry stood there with a pitcher of orange liquid and heat in her face.

"Martinos can choose one of the other rooms," Cherry said.

A wave of liquid sloshed over the top of the pitcher as she set it on the round table. She made a tsking sound under her breath and filled two glasses before bustling away. She returned with a cloth to wipe up the spill.

"Joanna, wash your hands, then come and take a seat. I'm making sandwiches."

"Yay!" Joanna skipped through the doorway and disappeared. Five minutes later, she appeared, still hopping and leaping, her ponytail bouncing. She danced around the table and slid into the seat next to him. She carried a book with her. "Do you like to draw? I do. It's my favorite thing."

"I enjoy painting," Martinos said. "Can you show me your sketchbook?"

"After lunch," Cherry said firmly.

"After lunch," Joanna conceded. "I've been drawing dragons today. It's hard because I haven't seen one. Mummy described them to me, but she said dragons aren't real."

Martinos presumed dragons had passed into myth and legends here on the mainland. But he was a talented artist or had been in his day. "I will show you how to draw a dragon."

"Let Martinos rest and eat first." Cherry bit her lip and shot him a glance.

"Does that mean you trust me now?"

"You're still a work-in-progress," she retorted.

Martinos laughed, a burst of humor right from the gut that hurt his side as it pushed free. It was one of the few times in memory he'd issued a natural response.

"Ham sandwiches okay?"

"I don't know what a sandwich is," he said.

"You eat meat." She leaned closer to whisper in his ear. "Do they have dragons who just eat vegetables?"

"No." He barked out another laugh at the very idea. Not in his family home. Not when he'd been a child. His father enjoyed a side of beef while his mother favored young goat. "I'll eat whatever you give me. Any food will be a treat." And that was nothing less than the truth.

A sandwich, he discovered, was slices of bread with a filling between—pinkish meat, sliced thin. Cherry had partnered it with vegetables and a spicy yellow sauce. He and Joanna munched through a plateful of the sustenance. Cherry produced a sweet pie that she told him was apple, and they demolished that too. Joanna finished with another glass of juice while Cherry made a pot of tea.

"Thank you. That was delicious." Martinos covered his mouth to hide his yawn.

Cherry stood. "Joanna, you need to have a nap."

"Mr. Martin said he'd draw a dragon for me to copy," Joanna said, her tone a trifle whiny.

"After your nap," Cherry said. "Martinos needs to have a rest, too, after I check his ribs."

"Oh," Joanna said.

"If you're good, I'll read you one quick story before you go to sleep," Cherry said.

"Okay. May I be excused?"

"Yes. I'll be there in a few minutes."

Joanna skipped away, and Martinos couldn't hide his amusement.

"Let me show you the shower and the bedroom. I'm afraid you'll have to don the same clothes, but perhaps you can purchase items on the mainland tomorrow. We'd have to check the tide to see what time the causeway will be open."

"I don't have any money," Martinos said. "I'll make do."

"Leave your clothes outside the door, and I'll wash them. By the time you wake, they should be dry."

"You are very kind." He was lucky her attitude was shifting to trust. He vowed not to let her down.

"Let me clear the table, then take off your shirt. Does anything feel broken?" She clapped a hand over her mouth. "Popsicles, I should've asked you that earlier."

"My ribs are bruised and shouting their distress. My feet are sore. I've cut them while walking barefoot."

"Then a hot shower will help. Off with your shirt." She gestured at him, her cheeks going pink again.

It hurt to lift his arms, and she had to help him raise the garment over his head. Her hand trembled a fraction before her fingers settled on his ribs. She pressed gently.

"Does that hurt?"

"A little."

"The graze isn't deep. You'll live."

She lifted her hand, and contrarily, he wanted it back on his flesh.

"Let me clean these." She peered closer. "No, wash your scrapes and wounds while you're in the shower. Let's see your feet."

Obeying an instinct, Martinos placed his hands on her shoulders. She froze, her gaze flying to his. The tiny sound she made turned him watchful. He studied her face, his interest zoning in on her full pink lips.

"What?" she whispered, her voice lower and throaty.

"I have an urge to kiss you."

Her throat worked in a hard swallow. "An urge? Ah, that's not—"

"A strong one," he added. "But I will wait until a later time."

She pulled her full bottom lip between her teeth while her gaze remained connected to his. He leaned closer and heard her audible inhalation of breath.

"Um, I'd better read Joanna her story." She fled and disappeared through the door.

Martinos wanted to whistle. A warm sensation spread through his chest, and he realized it was happiness—an emotion he hadn't experienced for a long time.

He had no money, no plan, no idea what he should do, yet the hours spent with Cherry and Joanna had been the best in his living memory.

It was the simple things: conversation regarding trivial matters and food, clean water.

Peace.

He never wanted to leave.

No sooner had the thought formed than he accepted reality in its place. Somehow, he had to return to the Dragon Isles. Nan and Leo's brothers were up to something, and he suspected innocent dragons and humans might suffer if Nan and her cohorts got their way. Then there was his dragon. Martinos couldn't continue without his other half. While he'd initially decided on gaining revenge, learning the truth might suffice. Meeting Gwenyth and now Cherry had helped him understand he had a life to live.

Cherry had mentioned the abbey. If there was an abbey, there must be druids. He added *find a druid* to his mental list—one skilled in magic who might reverse the spell keeping his dragon inert.

Not a tall order. He could do that with his hands tied behind his back. Martinos made a scoffing sound and pushed to his feet. He limped inside on unsteady legs and hobbled along the short hall Cherry had mentioned. He could hear Cherry reading Joanna a story, her voice changing for the different characters as she read. Joanna's sweet giggle brought a wash of contentment.

Martinos found the bathroom. He closed the door and stripped off his clothes before leaving them outside the door. He shut it again with a click. Cherry had told him to use the towels on the rails. Although a part of him hoped he couldn't operate the water and required help, he found the shower easy to work. Martinos stepped beneath the flow.

Warm water. A luxury since his ablutions in the dungeon had been limited to a bowl of water he collected himself.

He used the soap in the shower dispenser and lathered up his chest. Next, he washed his hair and beard before cleansing his scrapes and bruises. A few cuts on his feet were deep. He winced as he wiped the dirt off a scratched toe. He'd need to take care not to get them infected.

Once clean, he felt refreshed and lighter. He dried his hair and body and wound a towel around his waist before leaving the bathroom. His clothes had disappeared, so he returned to the table and chairs outside. Martinos's eyes drifted closed, and he edged toward sleep, lulled by the sun on his body. His time in the dungeon had taught him to grab rest whenever he could, since he'd never known when the guards might prod him awake to taunt him.

Here, at least, he was safe.

CHAPTER 6

Dragon Trapped in a Human Body

Cherry finished reading Joanna a story concerning a dragon that hoarded its treasure and had trouble with thieves. If Martinos was a dragon, did he have wealth? Something to ask him later.

The shower was still going when she scooped up Martinos's clothes from outside the bathroom door. Once she'd dumped them in the washing machine, she cleared away the lunch dishes. If Martinos stayed with them for longer, she'd need to pop over to the mainland to purchase more food. She scowled at a dirty plate, her hostess self battling with her protective responsibilities for Joanna.

Better to stay hidden as much as possible. Keep away from busy public areas to avoid the likelihood of Tony spotting them.

As she wiped the counter, she pondered her options and, as she often did, turned to her books and reading for a solution. Cherry considered the recent mysteries she'd consumed. She straightened as an idea occurred. Perfect. When she drove to the mainland, she'd wear a hat and casual clothing—items different from her standard attire. A T-shirt. Yes, not even her mother would recognize her if she wore a casual T-shirt with a feminist saying. She grinned. No, one a tourist might choose to wear. With Joanna, she'd make a game of the disguise. She and Joanna could write a detective story with camouflaged characters. *Huh!* And her mother worried Cherry's life was dull.

Untrue.

Her phone rang. This time, she checked the caller's identity. Never let anyone say she was stupid enough to make the same mistake twice.

"Rena," she said.

"I fell asleep on the couch," Rena blurted. "Had another dream."

"Right." Cherry waited for Rena to add details.

"It was a weird dream, but the robed man in my dream reiterated that if you come across a man on the beach—possibly injured—you should trust him. He's telling the truth. You have to help him because it's part of the big plan, whatever that means.

Your part is important."

Cherry's hand tightened on the phone as she listened to Rena while her mouth dropped open. Shock. A hint of surprise. Amazement. Each of the emotions whirled through her mind and sank to her gut. Slowly, she rotated her stance toward the bathroom and stared as if she could see through walls. This was plain weird. Popsicles weird, but at least her urge to trust both Rena and Martinos was right.

"He kissed me," Rena blurted.

"Who kissed you?"

"The man in my dream. He kissed me, and it was the best one I've had all year. Am I going bonkers? Why is this guy in my dreams? He's so persistent, and when I'm in the dream, everything makes sense. I mean, who on earth walks up to a guy on a deserted beach and trusts him enough to take him home? That's madness."

"Rena." Cherry attempted to break into the conversation.

"No sensible woman. Not a one."

"Stop. Let me talk."

"Sorry. I've drunk four cups of coffee this morning. I woke up feeling as if I hadn't slept a wink. Who knew dreams could be so exhausting?"

"Rena!"

"Yes?"

"I've met the guy on the beach. He told me he's a dragon shifter, and he's from a place called Dragon Isles."

"What?" Rena blurted, her shock clear. "My dream has come true?"

"He's taking a shower at this very moment."

"Dragons take showers?"

"Yeah. So it seems."

"Are you freakin' kidding me? You picked up a strange man? With Joanna at your side?" Rena burst out, sounding slightly deranged.

"You told me to do it. You're the conduit for the info. Besides, despite the dragon business, he sounds creditable. You didn't see the way he looked at Joanna—as if he recognized her."

"Yeah, but... This is crazy."

"You kissed a strange man," Cherry shot back. "You've had sex with your man."

"In my dream."

Cherry laughed, and her chuckle emerged with an edge of hysteria. "Call me stupid, but we're not in Kansas anymore."

"If a tin-man comes along, I'm outta here," Rena muttered.

There was a pause before Cherry spluttered out a giggle, and Rena joined in, still sounding crazed.

"What's the dragon like?" Rena asked once they'd ceased their strained amusement.

"He's gorgeous, and he's tried very hard to make me feel as if he's not a threat. What I don't understand is how your dream man knew."

"No idea. This woo-woo stuff is beyond me. I'm coming to the island," Rena said. "Strength in numbers."

"Is Tony still hanging around, or has he given up?"

"He threatened to call his lawyer. Again. I told him to go ahead. We have temporary custody of Joanna until the judge decides otherwise."

Cherry frowned. "The last thing we want is to face cops or lawyers. What if Tony goes to the cops and creates another fuss? Sneak away, so Tony can't focus his frustration on you. I mean, what if he follows you here and snatches Joanna? Once he has her, we'd have trouble getting her back. She needs stability right now until we know..." Cherry trailed off. Saying the actual words—that her best friend, Rena's sister, had drowned after her car sailed over the edge of a cliff—made everything seem final. Irreversible.

She preferred the dream man's version of Liza still being alive.

Rena snorted. "Greed drives Tony. I don't get how such a charming and personable man can act with such callousness. He cares nothing for Joanna. He sees her as a tool to bleed money from Dad and Liza. But I agree with you. I'll sneak away, even if it means a disguise or I have to skulk through the backstreets. I'll call you once I'm close to the island."

"Will you bring your vehicle?"

"No, I checked on the internet. There's a bus I can catch. I'm positive Tony has someone watching the apartment. If I ring a girlfriend and we go shopping on foot, Tony won't stress. He treats women as empty-headed vessels. Once I'm out of the house, I can catch a bus or hitch a ride."

Cherry tensed, tightening her grip on her phone. "You can't hitchhike! It's dangerous."

"Chill. I have two friends who will help if I ask. All I need to do is ditch anyone who follows me." Rena sounded confident, but Cherry suspected evading Tony would require skill and luck.

"When will you come? Tomorrow?"

"I'll pack now and try to get closer to Holy Island. Perhaps I can stay at a hostel—a place below Tony's lofty standards. I'm not sure if I can book a bus ticket online. That'd be easier."

"Be careful, Rena. Don't push Tony too far."

"Pooh," Rena said, and Cherry imagined her wrinkling her nose. "Tony is so arrogant it makes him stupid. I'll call you tomorrow morning as soon as I confirm my plans. You take care of the dragon. Bye."

Rena hung up before Cherry could caution her further.

"Is something wrong?"

Cherry jumped and let out a strangled *eep*. She pressed her phone to her chest, her heart battering her ribs as she turned to face Martinos. "You gave me a fright."

"My apologies," Martinos said.

It was then Cherry registered his partial nakedness. His skin was pale as if he hadn't seen the sun for months, and while he was thin, his chest was broad as if he normally possessed more muscle. She glimpsed his tattoo again—low his belly. His dragon still curled in a tight ball, and an air of depression radiated from the sleepy red figure. The towel wrapped around Martinos's waist concealed the dragon's feet and tail. Aware her attention had slipped dangerously close to Martinos's groin, she ripped her gaze away to stare at his beard. "Did you need something?"

"I was wondering about my clothes."

"They're still washing," Cherry said. "You look tired. Rest, and by the time dinner is ready, your clothes will be dry. We can buy you something else to help you blend when we go to buy food tomorrow."

"Thank you. Do you have a chew-stick I can use?" Martinos pointed at his teeth.

"A toothbrush?"

He stroked his beard, and Cherry didn't think he recognized the term.

"To clean your teeth," she elaborated. "You're in luck. I have an airline one in my purse for a backup. You can use that, and we'll get you one when we go shopping." She hesitated, then explained what to do with the tiny tube of paste that came with the toothbrush.

"Thank you again. It is a luxury feeling so clean. When can we visit the druids?"

She recalled their earlier conversation. "Oh, you mean the abbey."

He gave a clipped nod, his brows drawn together, expression anxious.

"I've checked the tide. We'll have time for an abbey visit before low tide tomorrow. Once it's safe to drive over the causeway, we'll have several hours to fill until the tide is low again."

Martinos frowned. "I overheard you. Will Joanna be in danger?"

Everything in Cherry softened on hearing his concern for Liza's daughter. "I'll try to disguise her and my appearance, but Rena says Tony is still in the town where we live. She intends to evade him and join us here on the island."

Martinos watched her closely. "Is there more?"

Cherry puffed out a breath, her cheeks rounding with the action. "Rena has had weird dreams. I'm not sure how long she's been having them, but she dreams of a robed figure. He told her we'd meet on the beach, and I should look after you."

His eyes widened with eagerness rather than surprise. "A druid? They're known for their divination skills. Sometimes, they just know. My parents used to pay one of the druids to help them with business decisions."

Cherry shrugged, still bemused. "You can ask Rena for details when she arrives, hopefully, tomorrow." Cherry paused, her curiosity burning with questions. "Can you tell me more about what happened? How you got the armband?"

"It's a painful tale," Martinos admitted, his features turning stark. "I'm worried the truth will make you fear me, that you will cease to help me. I have no resources and no friends on this side of the barrier."

Cherry quashed the uncertainty that came with his words and shoved it away. No, she needed to keep an open mind.

"Sleep first. We'll talk once Joanna goes to bed." She studied his chest for a moment before directing her gaze back to his chin or what she could see of his jawline. "I can't concentrate on serious matters when you're half-dressed."

He blinked, his harsh features softening in a grin—a slow widening of his lips, a flash of humor that twinkled in his brown eyes. "If it's any consolation," he said in a slow drawl that had her breathing faster and every feminine hormone jumping to attention, "I struggle to concentrate when you're in the same room."

Her brows climbed her forehead while she had trouble holding his gaze. "Oh," she said because she should say something.

"Later is fine. I'll admit, I'm exhausted." With that, he turned away.

Cherry ogled his butt as he left and tried not to let her imagination stray too far from decent. She failed.

Several hours later, once Joanna was in bed for the night, stories read, and her doll tucked up beside her, Cherry picked up a bottle of wine and two glasses before directing Martinos to the outside deck.

Since it was late summer, almost autumn, they were lucky to

have the balmy weather they'd been experiencing this week. She intended to make the most of the warmth before gray skies and drizzle became the norm and drove everyone indoors.

"I figured this might be a heavy conversation, so I've brought wine." She slid onto one of the deckchairs. Not quite dark, it was peaceful with none of the traffic noises or sirens that were part of everyday town life. The first hours here, the silence had bothered her. Now, with Martinos at her side, she found the quiet more palatable.

"Where do you want me to start?" Martinos asked.

"Wherever you think is best."

He nodded and accepted the glass of red wine she poured him. She watched him sniff the contents before he sipped. He supped again before placing the glass on the wooden table between their chairs.

"I was born on Smoking Isle, the oldest son of the ruling family. The heir. My sister Nan came along the next year. As a child, she craved the limelight, and over the passing years, her need for power grew. Her ambition. We had friends in common. Leo's older brothers, for instance—Leo is the dragon who helped me escape. One night we visited a new pub, but it turned out, it was a trap. Nan and Leo's brothers—my so-called friends—set me up with a woman. They put something in my drink that knocked me out. I knew what I was doing, but my reactions were sluggish. Whatever it was turned my dragon giggly, and he is not the giggly type."

Cherry nodded, her inquisitiveness regarding dragons increasing. Nothing alarming so far, but she sensed Martinos's story might take a turn for the worse.

"My friends attacked the woman." He closed his eyes. "I could do nothing to help. Someone hit me on the head, and when I woke, I was in a popular lodging house, naked and in bed with the woman. She came to and, on seeing me, screamed in terror. Men and women came running. The sheets were bloody. Blood covered the woman's lower body, and she shook violently, petrified of me while I was plain confused. I had an excruciating headache, and the drug made me sluggish. The authorities arrested and charged me with the crime. Because I was the heir, the justice sent me to the dungeon on Hissing Isle rather than on my home island.

"I suspect my sister wanted me out of sight and out of mind. I've been in the dungeon for three years and thought I'd die there."

"What changed?" Cherry asked.

"Gwenyth arrived. I mentioned her earlier. As I told you, the guards placed her in the cell next to mine. We talked, became friends. When Leo came to rescue Gwenyth, she persuaded him to set me free. Nan, my sister, wasn't happy with Gwenyth's arrival. Nan manipulated the situation, so Gwenyth was to go into the arena and fight."

"What?" Shock punched Cherry in the gut. Surely she hadn't heard correctly.

"Sometimes, in the past, to celebrate a special event, we had pit battles where prisoners fight animals and each other. The eventual victor wins a pardon, which is a tremendous incentive for everyone to fight to the best of their abilities."

"They intended to place a human woman into this fight," Cherry said faintly.

"Yes."

"With the expectation she'd die during the fights."

"Correct," Martinos said.

"You?"

"I'd have landed up in the fight pit too."

"That's barbaric."

"Yes," Martinos agreed. "While the fights aren't outlawed, the event hasn't taken place for at least twenty to twenty-five years. We were lucky to escape beforehand."

"Your sister sounds awful." Cherry slapped her hand over her mouth, consternation widening her eyes as she stared at Martinos. Well, that was tactful.

Martinos chuckled. "Don't worry. There's no love lost between my sister and I. I was young and stupid. The years in the dungeon have given me time to think and a reason to change. Once I get back to Smoking Isle, I'll do things differently."

Cherry took a sip of her wine. "Different how?"

"First, I'll check on what my sister has been up to because she had a reason for her machinations. I get that she wanted to run the family business, but as much as I've racked my brain, I don't understand what else she might've had in mind. I must learn what she's done, and how the humans on Smoking Isle are faring."

"Why is it called Smoking Isle?"

"We have an active volcano on the island. Most days, a plume of smoke rises from the vent at the top."

"What are the other islands called?"

"Perfume Isle and Hissing Isle." His eyes gleamed with silent humor as he waited for her response.

"Why are they called Hissing Isle?"

"The island has hidden caves that make strange noises with the rising and retreating tides, plus most of the beaches consist of small pebbles. They make hissing sounds when the waves rush into shore. Perfume Isle is home to many fragrant trees and plants. Spices and herbs," Martinos said.

"And dragons live side-by-side with humans."

"Not exactly," Martinos said. "The dragons make the rules and allow humans to live on the isles."

"I see." The dragons lorded it over the humans and made them feel like crap.

"From what I understand, Leo has dealings with the humans, but most dragons ignore them and only pay attention if they serve a use."

Cherry scowled. "Why do they remain with the tension between your races?"

"The humans have nowhere else to go. When the druids

conducted their magic and made the isles invisible to those on the mainland, the humans became trapped."

"Did they have a warning?"

"Yes, but many were refugees or in trouble with the law. They had limited options. Life isn't too dreadful for humans. Most live in comfortable houses and run businesses. Not all dragons disparage them."

"Your home sounds unpleasant," Cherry said.

"Do you not have trouble in your world?"

Cherry opened her mouth to deny problems then halted. Life wasn't perfect here either. "Every place has advantages and disadvantages." Tony, for instance, fitted into the problem category. The man was a leech, intent on sucking Liza dry. "Do you think your Gwenyth could be my friend Liza?"

"I'm not sure." Martinos appeared grave. "I hate to raise your hopes. The description you gave of your friend resembles Gwenyth. She speaks similarly to you and is a human, but her name was Gwenyth, not Liza. Leo was protective of her. Leo's dragon has accepted her as his mate."

"Mates? I thought—" Cherry broke off, embarrassed by what she'd intended to say regarding fated mates. Most males—men—treated her like a ninny when they learned she enjoyed reading romances. Her last date had sneered at her, so she'd walked out on him before she'd even ordered dinner. He'd chased after her and demanded she pay for her drink. When she'd stepped back into the restaurant, everyone had stared. Her cheeks heated at the memory.

"What did you think?"

Cherry sucked in a fortifying breath. "I own a bookstore," she said.

His brows rose, drew together. "Yes."

"I enjoy reading."

"I used to read," Martinos said, still sounding puzzled.

"My favorite books are romances and mysteries."

"Yes?"

Cherry's prickliness faded. "Many authors use the fated mates trope when they write their romances. I didn't realize the mates concept was real."

Martinos grinned. "It's the stuff of fiction in my world too, but Leo and Gwenyth *are* mates. The connection between them is strong. It's heartening." He captured her gaze with his. "Most dragons join their lives with another for practical reasons. My parents had no care for each other. Their marriage was a business venture. Successful in one way since they had a male heir. The attempt for a spare didn't work out since they had Nan. After that, they gave up and took lovers whenever the urge struck them."

Cherry frowned, the romantic in her hating the practicality in his voice. His acceptance of the idea. "Is that what you want?"

"While I was in the dungeon, I planned how to escape and my revenge. Now that I'm free, apprehension and indecision unsettle

93

me. I don't know what I want. I feel as if I've missed half the story."

Disappointment seared Cherry. She wanted love. That one special person who loved her for what and who she was, warts and all. She craved this type of relationship. Her mother had told her she was too fussy, that her steady diet of romances had given her unreasonable expectations. She disagreed, refused to settle for less than passion, respect, shared interests and goals. A man who didn't expect her to exist on meals of lettuce leaves.

Martinos gave her a slow smile that made his eyes glow with warmth. A sexy grin that had heat rushing through her body and sinking between her thighs. "After seeing Leo and Gwenyth together, I will take more care when I feel the urge to take a life partner."

"You don't think their regard for each other made them weak." Cherry held her breath as she waited for his reply.

"Leo cares deeply for Gwenyth. He loves her. Leonidas is Champion of the Skies. He's a dragon who wields significant power because of his title. Despite this, I've never heard tales of him exploiting his position. From what I picked up from the guard's gossip, he keeps to himself and seldom visited the castle lorded over by his family. Everything he has he earned without the help of his parents. Leo strides through life to the beat of his own drum."

Cherry sighed at his words. "Leo sounds like a hero in a romance."

"If it wasn't for Gwenyth—Leo wanted to leave me in the

dungeon. He didn't trust me or my assertions of innocence. Leo and Gwenyth made me want to be a better dragon. A fair one and a leader rather than an arrogant overlord."

"Are your parents still alive?"

"As far as I know, but my sister is in charge. I'm not sure how she managed this feat, but she has always possessed ambition along with slyness and the ability to get others in trouble for her misdeeds. There was a time when we were close, but no longer."

"I try to have an open mind, but given what you've told me, your sister isn't an agreeable person. Ah, dragon."

"You believe me?"

Cherry grinned. "I'm exercising my open mind."

"Fair enough."

"What will you do?"

"Hopefully, if I can find a druid, he can remove the bracelet to free my dragon. Then, I need to return through the barrier to Smoking Isle and regain control. I'm determined—no, honor-bound—to undo any damage my sister has wrought on our people."

"You'll have to face-off with your sister."

Martinos grunted. "Not something I'm anticipating with eagerness."

"What will you do to her?"

Martinos scowled. "Knowing Nan and with what I've heard over the years, it will come to life and death. One of us will die."

Shock pummeled Cherry again. "Is your world so brutal?"

"It can be."

"If Liza is in your world, I hope she is alive and safe. That she's doing okay. Joanna—" Cherry's voice cracked, and she broke off to clear her throat. "Joanna needs her mother. I don't know what will happen if Liza is d-dead. The courts might decide Joanna's father has the right to full custody. Tony is a selfish man. So greedy. He'll use his daughter as a pawn to gouge money from Liza's family."

"Your friend has a family?"

"A father. Liza's father remarried after he divorced Liza's mother and returned to England from New Zealand. Liza has a half-sister, Rena. You'll meet her soon since Rena is coming to Holy Island."

"What's a divorce?" Martinos asked.

Surprise had her turning to him. "When a married couple decides they are no longer compatible, they can get a legal grant to dissolve their wedding vows. You don't have this?"

"No, once a couple joins, they are a couple for life."

"What if they come to hate each other?"

"They live separate lives."

"So, your Leo and Gwenyth are partners forever?"

"Their case is unique because the dragon bonds with them both. A love match. For a dragon to bond, the creature harbors no doubts. According to legend, their bond is strong and unbreakable."

"Wow."

"Yes," Martinos agreed. "I envy them. I'd give anything for my dragon to move naturally. When the druid bound him, it felt as if I were only half alive. I still feel adrift," he confessed. "It's hard to explain the loss."

Empathy had Cherry reaching for his hand. The moment her fingers met his callused palm, a spark of awareness had her gasping. Martinos groaned, and she met his gaze. "What happens if you can't return to your home?"

Martinos slumped for an instant before a fierceness took possession of his stark features. "There must be a way. I arrived here, so there must be a way to leave. If not..." He shrugged. "I guess I'll adapt and make an alternative life here."

Cherry barely prevented her physical reaction, but pleasure and excitement poured through her mind. Although they'd known each other for such a brief time, she liked him a lot. She trusted him and his crazy *truths*, which was saying something.

She was in big trouble and smart enough to admit it.

CHAPTER 7

Time For a Disguise

Cherry slept late after tossing and turning for most of the night, her mind busy with everything Martinos had told her.

Dragons.

She and Liza discussed the mystical creatures often, given Liza was writing her book. Each new myth Liza uncovered thrilled them both.

She trudged into the en suite and ran the water until it turned warm. With her face washed, her fatigue lifted, and she rapidly dressed. As she headed for the kitchen, she could hear Joanna chatting in her little-girl voice. She found Martinos sitting at the breakfast table with Joanna. She was eating her cereal, and there was surprisingly little mess. Martinos cradled a mug in his big hands, and he appeared more rested than Cherry.

This morning, despite his scraggly beard and long hair, he looked good. His eyes were brighter, and he held himself upright with more confidence. His masculinity pulsed from him, and once he regained weight and tidied his hair and beard, he'd turn the head of every woman in the vicinity. Her happiness dispersed a fraction. Once that happened, he'd have his choice of women. She wouldn't warrant a second glance.

"Uncle Martinos helped me with breakfast. I showed him what to do," Joanna chirped.

"You did," Martinos said, his face softening. "The coffee is hot. Joanna assures me you don't eat breakfast. Is that true?"

"I'm hungry today after our long walk yesterday. Why don't I make us eggs and toast?" Joanna's honorary title for Martinos didn't surprise her since Liza insisted on respect for those who were older.

Joanna turned to Martinos. "Do dragons eat eggs?"

Cherry opened her mouth to intervene despite the mushy warmth trying to take her out at the knees. Men who enjoyed interacting with children and who treated them with respect always got her straight through the heart. Then she paid greater attention to the conversation, ready to take it into a U-turn. Joanna was a chatty kid, and the last thing she wanted was for word of a real, live dragon living on Holy Island to spread. Cherry was positive the consequences of his presence becoming public knowledge would stun Martinos. He'd not understand the potential outcome of those with higher power getting their grubby hands on him.

"I'm uncertain if dragons eat eggs. The stories I've heard say they enjoy meat most," Martinos said.

The tension seeped from Cherry's shoulders. She smiled at Martinos in approval. "Eggs and toast suit you? We don't have bacon or sausages, but we'll shop later today. Oh! I need to check on the tide too. We—or rather I—slept later than usual. I know I promised a visit to the abbey, but we can do that once we return. That way, we can take our time."

Disappointment flickered across Martinos's face, but to his credit, he didn't complain. He merely nodded his agreement. "Can I help?" He rose and strode over to join her at the fridge. "I want to learn as much as I can, so I fit in instead of standing out as a visitor."

Cherry smiled, appreciation and admiration filling her and brightening her mood. This dragon-man possessed more nous than most of the men she'd dated. Those men had forced her into adult shoes while they enjoyed acting the immature child. No contest compared to Martinos.

"That makes sense." What she didn't add was if he ended up stuck here, he'd need to blend long-term. "You can take charge of making toast." She handed him a loaf of sliced toast bread and waved him toward the toaster. "Stick a slice of bread in each slot and push the lever on the side until you hear a click. Are things very different here?"

"You have the tools to make your life easier. Our food doesn't come in packets and boxes. Our servants go to the market for fruit, vegetables, bread, cheese, and meat as we need it. When we're in dragon form, we'll sometimes hunt and use our fire to cook the meat."

"Enough to turn a girl into a vegetarian," Cherry muttered.

Martinos grinned, and it took years off his face. Charmed, Cherry returned the sentiment, her stomach flipping with longing. It was so easy to imagine a man—Martinos—with a woman. He'd treat her with care and respect. This rape—the charges—she couldn't believe him committing this crime against a woman. No sooner had this thought crystalized then she pictured Tony. He'd fooled Liza. Heck, the first time she'd met Tony Richards, he'd charmed away her reservations. Her smile died a quick death. She'd watch and learn and ask Rena more questions the next time they spoke.

"I'll do scrambled eggs," she said, pushing her mind away from her safety concerns. "How hungry are you?"

"Very," he said, and his stomach rumbled to reiterate his reply.

Cherry laughed. "We'll shop for extra food today. If we're lucky, we can find a farmers' market, and you can show off your bartering skills."

"The servants always purchased our produce. I've never shopped on my own and have no clue as to the procedure."

"No problem. You can carry the bags. But first off, we'll get you clothes and a disguise for Joanna. Err on the side of safety and make it difficult for anyone searching for us."

"I will protect you," Martinos said.

Cherry thought he might be joking or acting with chivalry, but his features displayed seriousness and determination.

He noticed her glance and puffed up with masculine indignation. "I might not have access to my full dragon powers, but I will let no one harm you or Joanna."

Cherry gave a curt nod and chattered her way through making the scrambled eggs. Martinos watched with close attention. "You can make the eggs tomorrow," she suggested.

"Yes," he said, and she wanted to laugh at his enthusiasm. With Martinos eager to soak up information and experiences, she might become a lady of leisure and have the time to lounge out in the sun and read without feeling guilty. Now that was a vacation.

Martinos watched Cherry as she climbed into a green metal box. Joanna clambered into the rear without his hesitation and announced to Cherry she'd clicked her seat belt. He tugged at the lever, and a door opened. With the slightest trepidation that he did his best to hide, Martinos slid onto the seat and swung his legs into the vehicle.

"There's a lever underneath the seat," Cherry said. "Pull it to move your seat and give more legroom. Fasten your seat belt too. This." She tugged on a small silver latch, and a belt came out from the wall of the metal box. She clicked it into another lock to fit a black band to her chest. When Martinos found himself staring at her bountiful breasts, he jerked his gaze off and fumbled for the lever she'd mentioned. His seat flew back, startling an unmanly shout from him.

Cherry giggled. "It always gives me a fright too."

Heat flooded his cheeks, but he sucked up his embarrassment. Losing his temper or snapping in impatience wouldn't help him to blend.

"Try the seat belt." Cherry pointed at the lever.

He managed the task without difficulty.

Cherry fiddled with something, and the metal box issued a growly rumble. This time, Martinos contained his startle, and when Cherry made it move forward, he relaxed. It wasn't as good as flying, but they traveled at speed. Under Joanna's direction, he opened a window to savor the breeze on his face.

The land was flat without the mountains and volcanoes of Smoking Isle, the jungles of Perfume Isle, or the pine forests and mountains of Hissing Isle. Few trees grew on the island, making the scenery dull. The other metal boxes they passed and the buildings of different sizes attracted his attention, though. He glimpsed numerous people as they drove through town, their clothing foreign to him with the vibrant colors and wide variation of styles. One building snagged his interest with familiar signs. "Is that a pub?"

"Yes, we can visit for dinner or lunch one day. We'll go once the tourists return to the mainland, so it's mainly locals present."

"I'd enjoy that," Martinos said. "Do you have ale here?"

"We do." Cherry grinned at him, and his pulse raced. An unfamiliar reaction and one he hadn't experienced for years until meeting Cherry. Attraction. He tamped it down and focused on the conversation.

"Joanna, Martinos and I decided we'd play a game. We will buy extra clothes and make ourselves look different. A disguise. Do you want to play?"

Joanna leaned forward to poke her head between the two front seats. Interest shone on her small face. Martinos prayed for Cherry's sake her friend remained alive because he hated to imagine this tiny human girl living with a man who didn't value her.

"Like the movies, Aunt Cherry?"

"Just so. Do you have an idea what disguise you'll choose?"

"I want to dress as a boy," Joanna said without hesitation.

Cherry blinked in obvious surprise. "You'd need to do something different with your hair."

"The hairdresser could cut it," Joanna said.

Cherry halted the metal box at the end of a line of metal boxes and turned around to stare at Joanna. "You've grown your hair for years."

"I'm tired of the boys pulling my ponytail," Joanna said. "It hurts. If my hair was short, they couldn't do that. They only pick on the girls with long hair."

Martinos listened. "Do I need to punch these boys on your behalf?"

"No," Cherry blurted. "We don't use our fists. We use our words to defend ourselves."

Martinos continued to listen since the ways of this world were different. He had much to learn.

"Why don't you think for longer? Once the hairdresser cuts your hair, you can't put it back," Cherry said.

"It will grow back," Martinos said. "Look at my hair. I used to have it short, but it has grown long."

"Are you getting your hair cut?" Joanna asked.

"If Cherry says I should," Martinos said. "Will my disguise need shorter hair?"

"I like your hair." A blush washed into Cherry's cheeks, the heat bringing her clear discomfort since she stared out of the metal box's window instead of meeting his gaze.

An answering warmth pulsed in Martinos, but he'd gained enough experience with females to hide his grin. She liked him, or at least his appearance. The feeling was mutual. He'd been lucky to find a woman whose heart was generous enough to help a dragon in need. To trust him, despite his confession that he'd been in the dungeon. He valued her belief in him and refused to betray her confidence.

"I want to be a boy," Joanna said from the back seat.

"All right," Cherry said. "We can do that, but you can't go around pulling girls' ponytails."

"Aw," Joanna said, appearing downcast. "But I can climb trees and throw rocks."

"As long as you're not throwing the rocks at people," Cherry said.

Joanna tapped him on the shoulder. "Uncle Martinos, can you teach me how to be a boy?"

Martinos glanced at Cherry and caught her amusement. "I can," he said, bewitched by this tiny girl. He'd never had contact with youngsters. Perhaps it was because Joanna reminded him of Gwenyth, but the child fascinated him. "I'll teach you a few things I did when I was your age."

"What?" Joanna demanded.

"Burping. Little boys enjoy burping," Martinos said with a teasing glance at Cherry.

Cherry's brows rose. "Really?"

Joanna giggled.

"The causeway is open. We can go now," Cherry said.

Martinos watched with interest as the line of metal boxes made their way across a wet path. Once they reached the mainland, he spotted a large sign stating the safe travel times for the day.

"Every year, cars are lost, and people need rescuing after they misjudge the timing to cross the causeway. People can walk across to the island by taking the old pilgrim's way if they want. The walk takes a few hours. We'll have time to shop, buy groceries, and do some sightseeing," Cherry said.

Martinos continued to watch everything around him. "Is all the land around here this flat?"

"We have plenty of hills and mountains farther inland. The coast is steep and has lots of cliffs." She blinked and wiped one eye.

Martinos suspected her mind had drifted to her friend and sought to distract her. "What sightseeing might we do?"

"I'm not sure," she said, her voice steadier. "Perhaps a walk, or we can visit castle ruins or an old church. It depends on how much time we have."

"I want to have my hair cut short," Joanna said. "Can I turn my style into a girl's hair later?"

"We'll talk to the hairdresser," Cherry said. "I'm buying a brimmed hat to cover my hair. We can buy you and Martinos a boy's cap."

"What do boys wear?" Joanna asked.

"What do they wear at school?" Cherry asked.

"A uniform," Joanna said.

Cherry laughed, but Martinos didn't understand the joke.

Martinos returned to scanning their surroundings and searching for danger. When they'd crossed the causeway, he'd seen few metal boxes, but now the number had mushroomed. "Does everyone own a metal box?"

"They're called cars or vehicles," Cherry said. "Not everyone has one, but most people use a car to move around the mainland. If you don't own a car, you can walk, take a bus, or the train. I'll point out the vehicle types as we see them."

"I fly." Losing this ability ached like a sore tooth. Until he'd lost his dragon, he hadn't appreciated everything he'd had. Never again would he take his life for granted. "Or at least, I did."

Cherry reached over and squeezed his knee. "We'll find a druid to remove your armband."

He nodded, her innocent comfort robbing him of speech.

The buildings grew in number until they lined the street. Lots of people—men, women, and children wandered along the road, several carrying bags or pushing children in wheeled contraptions. It was new to Martinos, and he soaked up the sights. The clothes. The hairstyles. The shoes. The different bags the people carried. He noticed the buildings contained huge windows, which were full of goods on display.

"Is this your market?" he asked.

"Our shops. I think the supermarket will interest you. Where do you buy your clothes?"

"We summon a tailor to come to our home. They bring a selection of fabrics with them. Once we decide on styles and cloth, the tailor takes measurements. He makes garments and delivers them once he completes them. My mother and sister call for the dressmaker."

"And haircuts? Shaving?"

"Our valets perform the tasks for us. A valet cares for our clothes and helps us to dress."

"We used to have servants to do that, many years ago, but these days most people dress themselves and look after their clothing. You'll see. If you have any questions, ask me when we're alone. I don't want anyone overhearing our conversation and inviting nosy questions. It might be dangerous for you if someone discovers you're a dragon. Our government—the people who run our country might take you into custody because you're different. That's the last thing you want."

"I agree," Martinos said. "I will try my hardest to fit in with the human world."

Cherry halted the metal box—no, it was a car—in an area set aside for vehicles. She paid for something called parking and placed a ticket inside where someone standing outside could see she was in the right place. Martinos made a note of his first question and followed Cherry and Joanna.

They stopped outside a brick building. The window display contained colorful yellow, purple and white bottles, and hairbrushes. A bell tinkled when they pushed through the door. A youthful woman with bright pink hair came to greet them. Was this color common among the human population? Another question for Cherry.

Cherry discussed Joanna's hair, and the woman laughed when Cherry told her about the hairpulling boys. She promised to cut Joanna's hair so that she could be a boy sometimes and a girl when she wanted to change.

"Martinos requires a trim," Cherry said, gesturing toward him.

"Your husband has gorgeous hair. It's thick, although it looks as if it needs a shape and a conditioning treatment. What about the beard?" The hairdresser screwed up her nose.

Unsure of what to say, Martinos remained silent and let Cherry speak for him.

The hairdresser filled the conversational gap first. "I could trim it." She cocked her head and narrowed her eyes while studying him.

"Yes, to both," Cherry agreed. "I might do a few other things while you and Joanna get your hair cut. I'll be back in an hour," she promised.

"But—" Martinos glanced at the woman and didn't want to admit that Cherry leaving him in this unfamiliar environment scared him.

"I'm counting on you to make sure Joanna behaves," Cherry

said with a bright smile.

"I'm always good," Joanna protested.

"You are, poppet. Okay then, you make sure your uncle behaves." She pointed at Martinos, so Joanna understood.

Joanna nodded, her smile brightening the room. "I will, Aunt Cherry."

The hairdresser laughed, amused at their byplay and teasing. *He could do this.* He'd survived three years in the dungeon with his sanity intact, so this hairdresser held no danger for him. He'd submit and wait until Cherry's return. She took her responsibilities seriously and wouldn't leave them for longer than necessary.

Cherry stemmed her merriment until she entered Marks & Spencer, a large department store beloved by the English. Martinos had held a panicked expression when she'd left the salon, leaving him and Joanna alone with the hairdresser. At least this way, she couldn't make a fool of herself by staring longingly at him. The dragon-man was too cute for his own good, even with the excess facial hair. She rebuffed her thoughts when they drifted toward imagining his appearance once the hairdresser finished with him. The hairdresser, on the other hand, had held a glint of interest in her eyes.

Cherry quashed the instant punch of jealousy.

She had no rights with Martinos. The man was desperate to return to his home, and she couldn't blame him. Cherry gave herself a stern lecture and set her mind to her task. Clothes for Martinos, a hat, and more casual attire for her, and boy's clothes for Joanna. She grinned and hustled to the children's department to select Joanna's clothes first.

It was over an hour later when she approached the checkout to pay for her selections. The chore had taken longer than it should because she'd mooned over her choices for Martinos. Too many romantic novels raising her expectations and her imagination, her mother would've informed her.

The assistant rang up her purchases, the total making Cherry blink. Luckily, she'd saved plenty for an emergency, and she figured this rated as one. She'd stress over money and saving once Martinos left, and her life returned to her habitual routine. She wrinkled her nose. Perhaps her mother was right, and she needed to change up her behavior.

Martinos's arrival had shaken and stirred her schedule in a big way. She wished she could keep him.

CHAPTER 8

Temptation Tiptoes into the Room

When Cherry struggled into the hairdresser salon, she'd steeled herself for what she'd dubbed The Martinos effect. She'd under-prepared.

"Do I look like a boy?" Joanna demanded, planting her hands on her hips and giving her attitude.

Cherry dropped her bags of clothes on the floor and circled Joanna as she studied Liza's daughter from all angles. "Apart from the pink dress, you look perfect."

Joanna peered into the closest bag of clothes. "Can I put on my boy clothes now?"

"She can change out the back if you want," the hairdresser said. "I've almost finished with your husband's hair. How do you like his beard now?"

The hairdresser had clipped Martinos's black beard, and it now hugged the shape of his face. He was breathtaking.

"Cherry?" Martinos asked.

"I hardly recognized you," she said truthfully. "You're so handsome. I'll have to fight off the local women." Once he ate enough to regain weight, he'd turn even more heads. He flashed a smile. Her compliment had pleased him.

Joanna tugged on Cherry's tunic top, a non-verbal hint to hurry. "Come on, then." Cherry led Joanna in the direction the hairdresser had indicated, which turned out to be the break room. She rifled through the bags and pulled out a pair of jeans, a striped blue-and-white T-shirt, and red sneakers. "Do you like these?"

Joanna's eyes lit up as she reached for the jeans. Cherry helped her dress, then produced a navy-blue cap.

"I'm too clean," Joanna protested.

"We'll fix that later. Let's see if the hairdresser has finished Martinos's hair."

The hairdresser set aside the blow drier and applied product to Martinos's hair with her fingers. Martinos met Cherry's gaze in the mirror's reflection.

"What do you think?" the hairdresser asked. "I took off some length, but it's still long enough to tie back. Your husband's hair is curly, and it sits well."

Cherry nodded and tried to conceal the thrust of lust and her racing heart. "It looks fantastic. So does Joanna's hair."

Cherry paid the hairdresser, barely wincing this time at the total. Martinos's trousers plus the T-shirt she'd found in the cupboard where they were staying still worked. He wouldn't stand out in the supermarket.

"Thank you," she said to the hairdresser.

Martinos took the bags of shopping from Cherry. "I promise to pay you back. Somehow," he whispered.

Cherry squeezed his arm. "It's fine. What do you think of our new nephew?"

Joanna giggled.

"Boys laugh or snigger," Martinos said. "And they walk with confidence."

"Can you show me?"

Martinos shoved his hands in his pockets and swaggered away from them. Cherry hid a giggle as Joanna bit her bottom lip and copied Martinos's assured strut.

"Well done," Cherry said. "I doubt your mother or friends would recognize you now." Memories of Liza brought a sharp pang to her chest. Her eyes stung, and Cherry sucked in a huge breath to stave off her tears. Crying wouldn't help in the slightest. Strength was what she required, for Joanna's sake. "Joanna, we need to give you a nickname," she said when she reached Joanna and Martinos. "What do you say?"

Joanna nodded with enthusiasm. "Call me Jo," she said. "That's a boy's name, but it's still my name too."

"Excellent plan," Cherry said. "Come along, Jo."

They unloaded the shopping bags and decided it was time for something to eat.

The stop at the teashop proved fun. Cherry noted that Martinos watched everyone and everything. He asked her whispered questions and carefully soaked up knowledge for the future while Joanna—no, Jo—practiced masculine behavior.

Finally, Cherry hurried them off to their next destination—the supermarket. Martinos pushed the shopping trolley, and Jo fetched groceries from the shelves. Cherry crossed the items off her list.

"I like being a boy," Jo whispered. "When can I get dirty?" Her brow puckered. "Do boys have bubble baths?"

"No one will know if you have a bubble bath," Cherry said. "You can still do that."

"Most boys don't enjoy having a bath," Martinos said.

Jo wrinkled her brow, her expression one of acute distaste, and Cherry's amusement escaped, growing into a wide smile. "We'll keep your nightly baths a secret."

With the shopping done, they carried the groceries back to the car. Cherry popped the frozen and refrigerated foods in a chiller bag she'd brought with them to keep everything cold. They had enough food to last them for two weeks and ingredients to make bread and cookies.

"Oh, look. A bookstore. What a gorgeous old building." Cherry studied the lines of the black-and-white timbered shop with the bay window. A display of a recent thriller release took pride of place, the books partly obscured by a *For Sale* sign.

"It's different from your bookshop," Joanna piped up. "Older."

"The building has charm and matches the others alongside it," Martinos said. "It reminds me of the ones in our village."

"It is pretty," Cherry said. She glanced at the time and saw they still had several hours to fill before the tide turned again. "We could visit the local church. Or go for a drive along the coast."

"The sea, please," Martinos said. "I don't know if I'll be able to sense the protective barrier, but it's worth trying."

"But even if it's open or you can get through, you can't fly. You nearly drowned last time."

"It was the rogue wave," Martinos said. "Big enough to upset even an expert swimmer."

"I can swim," Jo piped up from the back. A reminder that Jo was listening to their conversation, and they needed to take care of what they discussed.

"But it must be a long swim. What if you don't make it? What if you drown?"

Martinos sighed. "I won't give in to impulse."

"Promise?"

"Yes."

Cherry studied him closely, saw his sincerity, and eased out a breath. She'd hate anything happening to him. Also, she was in danger of falling under his spell. Already. It was happening again—her tumbling into deeper feelings when there couldn't be a future for them. *When would she learn not to let her romantic yearnings take control? Silly woman.*

Chastened, she unlocked the vehicle and slid behind the driver's wheel. "I can teach you to drive if you want. Or at least describe the process. My vehicle is an automatic, so it's easy to drive."

"Yes, please, Aunt Cherry," Jo said. "Boys know how to drive."

Cherry gave a startled laugh. "Fair enough," she said. "Pay attention, both of you." Once she'd made sure her passengers had buckled up, she started describing what she was doing.

The rest of the day passed quickly, and she enjoyed the simple conversation with Martinos while Joanna made her laugh with her insistence on practicing boyish traits.

Rena called while they were driving across the causeway. Cherry thrust her phone at Martinos. "You can practice something new. Push that button there, hold it to your ear, and talk to Rena for me. She knows who you are."

Martinos fumbled the phone, but he answered the call. "Hello?"

When Cherry glanced at him, she struggled to hold back her amusement. Given Martinos was coping with myriad novel experiences, he was managing well. Way better than she handled new skills.

"What does she say?" Cherry asked.

Rena must've heard Cherry because she started talking. Martinos nodded.

"All right," he said. "I'll tell Cherry."

"Push the red button," Cherry said. "That will end the call."

Martinos followed her instructions. "Rena told me she wouldn't be coming for a few days." He glanced back at Joanna. "I'll tell you the details later."

By the time they arrived at their cottage and unpacked the groceries, Joanna was tired from running around. Cherry decided to have an early dinner.

"Martinos, I'm sorry. I thought we'd have time to visit the abbey when we arrived home. We've exhausted Joanna. We can visit first thing in the morning."

"Of course," Martinos said. "You have other responsibilities besides helping me. It's important to keep Joanna safe. I understand this."

"Tomorrow, I promise."

Martinos nodded. "Can I help to make your meal?"

"I need to supervise Joanna in the bath before I start dinner preparations. Why don't you have a glass of wine while you're waiting? Watch television or listen to the radio. Do you remember how to turn on both?"

"Yes," Martinos said.

Cherry nodded and hurried off to join Joanna.

"Pretending to be a boy is hard work," Joanna said as soon as she spotted Cherry. "They run around. When do they stop?" She poked her temples. "My head hurts from doing the walk Uncle Martinos showed me. Boys take long steps."

"Well, don't worry. You only need to keep to your disguise when we're outside the cottage."

"No," Joanna said, her decisive tone reminding Cherry of Liza.

A pang struck her heart, and she had to swallow hard. "No, what?" she managed.

"If I don't keep practicing, I might forget when we walk outside. We're doing this so Daddy doesn't steal me."

This time Cherry's throat thickened, and she coughed to clear the obstruction. "I hope Rena and I are doing the right thing."

"I don't want to make Mummy unhappy," Joanna said. "Daddy makes her sad."

It'd appall Liza if she heard her daughter and realized how much her child understood. She and Rena needed to make sure whenever they discussed Tony, Joanna wasn't present.

"You shouldn't worry your handsome boy head over grown-up stuff," Cherry said.

"Some of the kids at school have two houses. They stay with their mothers and visit their fathers on the weekends." Joanna's tone was matter-of-fact and unconcerned. This was her routine and the standard of many of her friends.

Uncertain of how to handle the situation, Cherry changed the subject. "Let's get this bath underway. Although she didn't have bubbles, she had a bath bomb. "You get undressed, and I'll find a bath bomb for you. Don't get in until we test the water temperature, okay?"

Soon, lavender filled the air. Cherry supervised while letting her mind wander to the kitchen and Martinos. The man—he wasn't for her. Men of Martinos's ilk never took a second glance at women like her. Someone who verged on plump and liked to read.

For a moment, she heard Rena's strident tones ringing through her mind. *Grow a spine, girl.* She had curves, and she should flaunt them.

Cherry gave a decisive nod and straightened her shoulders. She wasn't mistaken in thinking Martinos sneaked glances in her direction. He seemed to enjoy her company. She'd take that and try to step away from the dingbat act and toward cool and confident.

"Do you want to dress yourself?"

"Yes, please, Aunt Cherry."

Cherry pulled out the plug to empty the bath and stood. "I'll be cooking dinner with Martinos."

"Yay! I'm hungry."

Cherry ruffled Joanna's shorter hair. "How does macaroni and cheese sound?"

"It's my favorite."

"I know," Cherry said.

When she arrived in the kitchen, she found Martinos had opened a bottle of wine and had two glasses ready plus an orange juice for Joanna.

"You told me you have servants where you live."

"We do, but since meeting you, I've enjoyed doing things for myself. I had plenty of time to plan. At the start, I thought I'd die in the dungeon, and I had regrets. Before, I was a spoiled son and, in my way, as terrible as my sister. Speaking with Gwenyth helped me to understand everything I'd been thinking for years. I aim to become a better dragon—one more like Leo. I intend to find my way in the world instead of relying on the wealth my parents grew and my privileged position.

"Wanting to change is admirable. We can always be better people," Cherry said.

"Where should I put these things?" He indicated the cans of beans and fruit and the box of breakfast cereal.

"Why don't we leave them in the box and push it into the bottom of the pantry? They won't spoil, and it will be easy to find things."

Cherry started cooking dinner, giving Martinos a running commentary as she worked and getting him to grate the cheese for her. Joanna clattered into the kitchen. She wore a brown T-shirt and a pair of sweatpants. Her tongue tucked between her teeth, and she walked in an exaggerated man-gait. She'd even done her hair, combing it back in the manner the hairdresser had suggested.

A wave of lavender wafted after her, and Cherry hid her flash of humor.

"Can you show Uncle Martinos how to set the table?"

"Yes," Joanna said.

"Too many new things inside my head," Martinos said and winked at Cherry. "Some info falls out."

Joanna's brow furrowed. "Didn't your mother teach you?"

"No," Martinos said. "I wasn't lucky enough to have a mother to show me things or an Aunt Cherry to explain when I didn't know how to do something."

Cherry's heart pumped out an extra two or three beats as she murmured a silent wow to herself. Martinos was so good with Liza's daughter. Thoughts of her friend, missing and presumed dead, knocked away the happy mush in her brain. She coughed to clear her throat.

"Who wants to grease the dish?"

"Me!" Joanna said.

"Martinos, you can stir the sauce. Let me show you what to do."

Martinos enjoyed the quiet evening with Cherry and Joanna more than any other night in his memory. Not even long-forgotten days and nights spent with fellow dragons and friends compared with the contentment he found in doing things for himself, such as learning the basics of how to cook.

Spending time with Cherry prompted him to become a better

dragon, as had his days and hours chatting with Gwenyth. It gave him an awareness of others and highlighted his past selfishness and poor attitude toward servants. He now understood Leo wanting to make his own way rather than counting on his family and their connections.

"Time for bed, Joanna. You need to restore your tank with sleep since we're visiting the abbey straight after breakfast," Cherry said.

"Can I take my sketchbook?"

"You can," Cherry said.

"Do boys draw pictures and paint?" Joanna asked, her gaze on him.

"Yes, remember, I told you I used to draw when I was younger."

"I'll share my sketchbook with you." Joanna ambled over to where he sat and kissed him on the cheek. "Good night, Uncle Martinos."

She disappeared, running along the passage with a loud boyish shout before he could react.

Cherry must've spotted his reaction because she smiled. "Joanna is an exceptional kid. She sneaks into your heart when you're not paying attention."

He nodded, unable to speak full sentences when shock and pleasure still ricocheted through him. Joanna wasn't the only one who had scampered into his emotions. He watched Cherry when her attention was elsewhere. Cherry considered others, and intelligence shone from her eyes. Her red hair held fire, especially when she walked in the sunlight. The light in her hair reminded him of his dragon.

By Lodar, he missed communicating with his other half. He lifted his T-shirt—one of the new ones Cherry had purchased for him—and studied his sleeping dragon. Each time he checked, the creature had curled into a tighter ball and slid lower on Martinos's belly.

He had to find a druid to help him remove the spell.

Soon.

If his dragon died, he wasn't sure how he'd survive, how his body might react. As soon as the druid had slapped on the band and chanted his magical words, Martinos had stumbled, weakness overtaking him.

The guards had laughed when he'd fallen to his knees in agony.

It had taken weeks, months, for his body to strengthen enough to compensate for his dragon's absence. The guards never fed him enough. Likely on purpose, and he'd had to force himself to exercise through pain to maintain his human half.

Now that he'd rested from his escape, he should resume his exercise regime.

Tomorrow.

Cherry returned and took a seat on the deck beside him. "Are you okay? You look worried."

"I'll need to start exercises to improve my strength. The extra food is helping, but with my dragon bound, I must condition my muscles."

Cherry frowned. "You should've told me. We could've gone to the mainland tomorrow instead of today."

"No, with my arrival, you required extra food, and Joanna needed clothes," Martinos said. "I understood. You have been very generous supplying items for me. I intend to repay you."

"Don't worry. Having you around *is* helpful. Tony will search for a woman and child since by now, he'll suspect Joanna is with me. Having a man around makes us look like a family." Heat blazed in her cheeks, and she fumbled with her wineglass, taking a large sip. "We'll visit the abbey ruins tomorrow. That will be a start for your search."

"Thank you. Few people would offer the help you have."

"Oh!" Cherry said. "I'm so silly. I'll do an online search for you. They might have a local library for research. If there are druids on the island, perhaps they advertise. I mean, what do druids do?"

"Magic," Martinos said. "They work with nature and embrace the seasons. The locals go to them for talismans, and sometimes they make salves and healing balms."

Cherry retrieved her phone. Martinos had learned most humans possessed one and always carried it on their person. She tapped several buttons, her forehead screwed up in a frown.

"Huh," she said. "No druids on the island, but there are several on the mainland. Not too far from the causeway." She pressed another button and held her phone to her ear. "No reply. There's an answerphone. I'll leave a message."

Cherry left her name and phone number and disconnected. "As far as I know, the abbey has been in ruins for several hundred years. What do you hope to discover there?"

Martinos heaved a sigh. "I'm not sure. I'm hoping I'll sense something or learn what steps to take to free my dragon."

"What about the local church? Do druids pray in church?"

"Perhaps," he said.

Cherry waggled the bottle of wine at Martinos. "More wine?"

"Thanks."

Cherry rose, took half a step to take his glass, and tripped over the shoes he'd kicked off. "Oh!"

Martinos caught her before she hit the wooden deck. She froze, blinking up at him with wide eyes. His arms tightened around her shoulders. Her breasts pushed against his chest while her delicate floral scent filled his senses. "Cherry," he whispered. "What would you do if I kissed you?"

"You want to kiss me?"

"Very much."

She swallowed hard. "I guess that'd be okay. I mean, you can kiss me."

Martinos drew her closer and fitted Cherry to his body. The sharp zing of pleasure took him by surprise, but it shouldn't have. He hadn't touched a woman for years and not one as desirable as Cherry. Their lips touched and parted for two long seconds in which they stared at each other before Martinos closed the distance between their mouths and kissed her again. Her lips tasted of the red wine. Sweet and tart and even better than he'd imagined.

He pulled back a fraction and pressed his forehead to hers. They were both breathing faster than average, and he desperately wanted to ask if she'd liked the kiss. Could he do it again?

"C-can you do that again?" she asked. "I mean, if you want to, of course." Delicate pink colored her cheeks, and she hesitated, her uncertainty showing in her eyes.

Her lack of confidence pulled at him. Made him want to make her feel better about herself.

"I want to kiss you again," he whispered. "You're gorgeous. Any man with half a brain would want to get his hands on you."

"Are you certain?"

Instead of a reply, he showed her with actions. He kissed her deeply with more confidence since she hadn't rejected him. His inner self cheered when her hands settled on his shoulders and clung. They explored each other's mouths and tasted, and this time, Martinos let his hands wander over her back. They came to a rest at the base of her spine. He hesitated a fraction, then gave in to the need coursing through him. All day, he'd ached to caress her bottom and test the curved flesh beneath his hands.

She started at the first light skim of his fingers and pulled her mouth from his to eye him with reluctance.

"That's not my best feature," she blurted.

"Oh? What is your best attribute?"

"My breasts are decent."

More than decent, but then so was her arse. Martinos chuckled when she wrinkled her nose, the expression cute. This close to her, he spotted a few freckles, the perfect target for his lips and tongue. "Should I tell you what I see when I look at you?"

"Y-yes?" It emerged as a question.

"I see a gorgeous woman with touchable curves. Curves enough to entice any red-blooded man or dragon. I see glorious hair that contains fire and stunning brown eyes that remind me of expensive brandy. I see full, kissable lips and cute cinnamon-colored spots that you try to hide. I noticed all of that before I dragged my weary bones out of the sea and spoke with you. You have a generous nature. You're kind to others, and you're an excellent teacher. You're a loyal friend."

"But men don't want those things. They want exciting and fashionable—someone sexy and uninhibited who loves to party. A woman who can add to a conversation. They want a woman skilled in bed. One without reservations. Someone open to excitement and adventure."

"Says who?" Martinos scoffed.

"An ex-boyfriend. I wasn't exciting enough for him. According to him, a bookstore owner was boring, and his friends laughed at him when they discovered my occupation. He got upset because I refused to sleep with him on the first date. I'm cautious. I prefer to get to know the person before I jump into bed with them."

"You haven't known me for long," Martinos said. "You let me kiss you." He pressed another quick kiss to her lips because he could, because she tempted him like no other.

She offered him a shy smile, her gaze meeting his for an instant before it flitted away. "It's different with you. So much has happened in such a short time."

He caught her peeking at him, and he delighted in her flush. Martinos sent her a wink and watched in fascination as the color in her cheeks deepened to rose-pink. "You saved me from drowning."

"You were in shallow water and lying on the sand. You would've been okay."

"But you were kind enough to save me from a human hospital. You've told me it's best not to stand out, and you're right. I'd hate to attract the wrong attention and get myself in bigger trouble than I am now."

"You're blending with the locals and tourists, although I hope the druid is discreet and not a blabbermouth."

"The druids I know are reticent." He hadn't even considered the religious men might not keep his secret.

"We have to take care."

"Yes," Martinos said, understanding her concern.

"Do you have a plan?"

"Not yet."

"I wonder if Rena has learned anything else. She dreamed about you."

"Is everything coming true in her dreams?"

"I'm not sure. I sense she's holding back." Her nose wrinkled in that cute manner again. "Rena is an open person. Sometimes, she speaks her thoughts without censure. She's not saying much. In fact, she mentioned sex, but she didn't go into detail. She acted almost embarrassed."

"Is she safe from this man?"

"Rena can take care of herself. You spoke to her. I'm positive she'll be okay on her own."

"Let's talk about something else," Martinos said.

"What?"

"Tell me why you think your backside is unattractive because from where I stand, it's perfect. When I'm in full health, I'm a sizeable man. I prefer to fuck a robust woman with healthy curves."

"Ah...pardon?"

He found himself grinning and leaned closer to steal another kiss. "What I'm saying, Cherry, is I'm attracted to you. I've discovered kissing you is exciting, and I intend to do more soon. That's if you're on the same page as me."

"Ah...maybe," she squeaked.

Martinos scooped her off her chair and settled her on his lap. Seconds later, he kissed her, using every bit of expertise. For one breathless moment, he thought his dragon twitched beneath his skin. He paused the kiss and rubbed his nose against Cherry's while he cataloged the sensations within his body. No, he was mistaken. He sighed and returned to kissing Cherry.

He'd count his blessings instead of worrying over matters beyond his control.

Chapter 9

Of Beer and Burps

A nticipation had Martinos leaning forward in his seat, gaze scanning the countryside as Cherry drove toward the abbey. They passed through the insignificant town before turning into a space full of cars. The vehicles sat within painted lines, and people of all shapes, sizes, and skin color wandered toward an entranceway. While he, Cherry, and Jo climbed out of the car, another larger vehicle pulled up at the far end.

"That's a bus," Cherry said before Martinos could ask. "It's full of children, so it looks as if it's a school trip from the mainland." She glanced at the timepiece she wore on her wrist. "I didn't think it was that late. The causeway must be passable. Let's move and get our tickets before the kids." She ushered Joanna, who wore her boy clothes with panache, in front of them, then linked her arm with his.

It was challenging to see Cherry's face since she wore a wide-brimmed hat to cover her hair, but satisfaction and contentment filled him at the physical contact. Although Martinos understood the purpose of the disguise, he mourned the loss of what was becoming a favorite view. Cherry's creamy skin with the cinnamon freckles, her red hair, and her brown eyes that reminded him of his father's favorite whisky tipple.

"Two adults and one child, please," Cherry said to a woman standing behind a counter. Cherry presented a card in payment, and Martinos started to voice the questions tickling his lips.

"How do—"

"One boy," Jo exclaimed.

Martinos smiled and placed his hand on top of Jo's cap, deciding to quiz Cherry over the plastic money later. "What should we see first, Jo?"

"Not sure," Joanna said. "I want to draw things."

Cherry accepted tickets from the woman, shoved them into her bag, and ushered them through another large gate. This allowed Martinos his first view of the abbey. Cherry had told him the building lay in ruin, but he'd underestimated the damage. A croak escaped him, one of disappointment. For the abbey to descend to this state, the druids had left hundreds of years ago. How the devil would he free his dragon now? He'd thought...*hoped* he'd locate a druid here at the abbey. Confidence had kept him moving toward his goal, but now...

"The druids live in a monastery on Smoking Isle," he told Cherry in an undertone. "A part of me expected to find the druids conducting their daily business. What do I do now?"

"The druid I left a message with hasn't contacted me yet." She slipped her hand into his and squeezed. "We'll get you home if we can't remove your armband. I promise. We won't stop searching until we're successful."

Jo had run ahead while they'd been talking, and now she sprinted back.

She grabbed their hands and tugged them toward a stone arch that rose above their heads. Long ago, builders had chiseled patterns into the stone, and while other parts of the building had broken away, the arch remained.

"Let's explore," Jo shouted. "Take photos, Aunt Cherry. Lots so I can draw things when I get home to show Mummy when she gets here. Uncle Martinos will want to sketch too. Take lots and lots."

Cherry released a choked sound at the request, but she nodded approval. Martinos reached for Cherry and gave her a quick hug of silent commiseration. It hurt Cherry to keep the secret of Jo's mother's accident to herself.

Martinos and Cherry trailed Jo as she peered through gaps in stone walls and studied the carvings and unique designs. In the distance, adults and groups of children did the same thing. Laughter floated on the air: excitement and high spirits. From here, he spotted another building on a hill, and he pointed it out to Cherry.

"That's the castle. We'll go there another day. Perhaps, later this afternoon, we should visit the spot where we found you. You might notice a clue we didn't earlier."

"Thank you," Martinos said, meaning it wholeheartedly. Without Cherry, navigating this world would prove taxing. Dragons never helped each other to advance, and the idea of assisting a human would never occur to most. Cherry hadn't hesitated to come to his aid.

"We need to explore the entire abbey," Cherry whispered. "I get you're disappointed, but maybe something will jog your memory or offer a clue as to what to do next."

"You're right," Martinos said. "I shouldn't have expected this to be easy when nothing else has come without a cost."

Cherry tugged him in the direction Joanna had headed. "On the bright side, a few marvelous things have happened. You met Joanna and me."

Martinos hugged her against his side for a second. "I did, and you've been generous with your help. I appreciate it, and one day will repay you."

"Don't stress over that. I like to think you'd help someone in the same way."

Martinos considered her words, interested that they ran in parallel to his thoughts. He fought the scowl attempting to dig into his features. He'd been a selfish dragon before his captivity. The years of isolation had changed him, and meeting Gwenyth and Leo had helped him to see he wished to leave that self-centered dragon behind. While he was determined to change and believed he was on the way to becoming someone decent, memories of his earlier years, and the way he'd treated servants and those he considered less, shamed him.

"What is the purpose of the carvings on the stones? Is this a form of druid communication?" Cherry asked, breaking into his unhappy memories. She pointed at several runes etched into stone pillars.

Martinos scanned them and understood their meaning without difficulty. "They are specific runes to scare away ghosts and Vikings intent on plundering riches. They keep those dwelling within the buildings safe."

"The Vikings came here hundreds of years ago and plundered religious items and treasure. I believe that's part of the reason the inhabitants deserted the monastery. It wasn't safe."

"That makes sense. We have descendants of Viking explorers who live on the Dragon Isles. Some became trapped behind the barrier and couldn't leave while others chose to remain."

"We've explored the buildings," Cherry said. "Let's walk the boundaries. We might find something to help you."

Martinos wandered after Joanna and Cherry. Cherry stopped to take photos with her phone. Martinos studied the landscape and the human children playing tag when their minders weren't watching.

Cherry's phone rang, and she stiffened as she answered the call. Martinos strode over to her, only relaxing when she smiled.

"Rena. Where are you?" She listened before speaking again. "Okay. I'll tell Martinos. You have the directions for the cottage. We'll stay on the island until you get here. We're fine for supplies. You take care." She hung up and searched for Joanna. She was busy watching a butterfly.

"Rena is in Edinburgh. She wanted to make sure Tony hasn't followed her before she heads over to Holy Island. She told me not to speak to the druid I contacted. He's a fake and makes potions for tourists for exorbitant prices. He can't help you."

"What do I do?" Martinos clenched his jaw to hold back his aggravated curses.

"Rena's druid is trying to reach us. He has the spell to break the armband."

"What? How does he know what I need?"

Cherry shrugged. "I don't understand any of this. Rena says her dream man tells her this while she is asleep. It sounds peculiar, but the dream man hasn't steered us wrong so far. We should trust him."

"Waiting is hard. So is placing my faith in a stranger."

Sympathy rolled off Cherry in her kind words and soothing tone, making Martinos feel worse. "I'm sorry."

"None of this situation is your fault."

Cherry's phone rang again. She glanced at the screen before she answered. "Hello?"

Martinos stepped close to hear.

"This is Samuel. You called and left a message."

"Thank you, but I'm sorry. I no longer need your services," Cherry said.

"Botheration," the druid replied. "You must've contacted my chief competitor. I knew I should've rung back last night, but I had to watch the grandchildren. Two boys, they are, and very active. They force me to keep my wits alert. Well, you have my number, should you change your mind. Goodbye."

Martinos caught Cherry's gaze as she spluttered out a laugh. Her gaiety was intoxicating, and he chuckled.

"I didn't realize there was more than one druid handy to the island. He sounded so ordinary. A man in charge of his grandchildren. I don't know why, but I expected druids to act holy and serious like a priest—unmarried and full of piety."

"They are that way in my world and hold great power. Our druids maintain the barrier between our worlds. If your friend is right, the second druid won't be real either."

"No." Cherry sobered. "I'm sorry."

"Not your fault."

"Come and see the butterflies," Joanna shouted, wind-milling her arms in her enthusiasm.

Martinos allowed Jo to tug him to the thicket where he stood watching the lemon-yellow butterflies flit from flower to flower. Cherry stood beside him, and he curved his arm around her waist to draw her nearer. Contentment flooded him, and for a moment, he imagined a future with Cherry. A child of their own.

His bubble of satisfaction burst almost immediately. Cherry loved her bookstore while he needed to get back to Smoking Isle to halt whatever tyranny his sister had set in motion. There was so much he needed to put right.

Their future was not together.

All he could hope for with Cherry was a temporary friendship.

A sharp pang dug into his chest, and for a breath-stealing instant, he imagined his dragon stirred. But no. It was the beat of his heart as he acknowledged the future—his future without Cherry at his side.

After their busy morning, they returned home for lunch. Cherry made BLT sandwiches and enjoyed having Martinos at her side, assisting her each step of the way. No other man in her life had ever helped with the small stuff—the everyday chores. And not one of them relished a task like making bacon, lettuce, and tomato sandwiches.

Martinos took delight in each new skill he mastered, and once he learned something, he moved on to the next challenge. Right now, he was learning how to cook bacon while she shredded lettuce and sliced tomato.

With the sandwiches made, they moved out to the deck to relax and eat their meal. A breeze had sprung up since the morning, but the garden and deck remained sheltered because of the tall hedges surrounding the rear lawn.

Cherry munched on her sandwich while recalling their kisses from the previous evening. She'd gone to bed alone but tossed and turned for much of the night, her body revved and aching. In the end, she'd used her fingers to get herself off, but the pleasure had been fleeting and not as fulfilling as usual.

Tonight, she decided.

Tonight, she'd ask him to share her bed. She liked Martinos, and he seemed genuine in his regard for her. He'd told her of his past without sugarcoating the charges against him when he could've lied. She'd never have discovered the truth. She and Martinos had separate goals, came from different worlds. Their friendship would be fleeting and temporary.

In the past, that might've bothered her.

This time, she was following her urges.

Yep, no matter how mortifying, she intended to seduce

Martinos.

Go her!

Cherry produced the plate of chopped fresh fruit she'd prepared, and the three of them demolished that too.

Finally, she patted her tummy. "I need to exercise. Why don't we walk to town? Maybe we can have ice cream for afternoon tea. We can check out the pub too." And she'd keep an eagle eye out for Tony.

Martinos leaned back in his chair. "Are you sure it's safe?"

"We'll be in disguise," Cherry reminded him. "Let's live dangerously. We'll still have time to walk on the beach later."

Joanna stood and yawned without covering her mouth. She tried to burp and failed.

Cherry worked hard to contain her laughter. "It's rude not to cover your mouth."

"Boys don't do it."

"Yes, they do," Martinos said. "My nursemaid smacked the back of my hand each time I yawned with an open mouth."

Cherry rose to take their dirty plates to the kitchen while listening to Joanna's questions regarding a typical boy's behavior. If Liza returned and wasn't dead, as the authorities presumed, she'd be aghast at her daughter's shenanigans. Probably even more shocked that her proper friend had allowed Joanna to cut her hair.

Heck, she was acting out of character in lots of ways.

And she wasn't sorry one bit.

Martinos set off with Cherry and Jo on the walk to the small township. Jo had Cherry stop to take photos of various things—flowers, an owl, a panoramic view—that Jo told them she'd enjoy drawing. The child's chatter might have annoyed him in the past. Now, a smile twitched at his lips while he savored Cherry walking at his side. He was possessive of her, starting to consider her his woman.

A dangerous reaction.

They walked for ten minutes before they reached the village. Men, women, and children piled onto a bus parked on the edge of the road. The doors shut as they walked past, and the vehicle chugged off toward the causeway. Half a dozen cars pulled out of a car park and followed the bus. The town emptied of people until only they and locals remained.

"Will an ice cream make me burp?" Joanna asked.

"No," Cherry said. "A soda might do the trick."

"Yes, please," Joanna said, looking absurdly thrilled at the prospect.

"Did you want to burp all the time?" Cherry asked him in a whisper.

"Yes," he said. "It's a little boy thing."

"Thank goodness they wear out of it," Cherry muttered.

Laughing, he opened the door into the pub and ushered through Cherry and Jo.

"Is it okay for us to have a drink with our son here?" Cherry asked the barmaid standing behind the bar.

The barmaid's thin brows drew together. "The tide is on the way in now. You won't have much time to get over the causeway."

"We're staying for a few nights," Cherry said.

"In that case, you're welcome to stay and have a drink in the garden out the back." The barmaid smiled, revealing gold in one of her upper teeth.

Humans kept their wealth in their teeth? How strange. Martinos stared but kept his questions barricaded as the barmaid asked them what they wanted to drink.

"A pint and a half of lager and one lemonade," Cherry said.

The barmaid poured the drinks, and Cherry paid for them.

"I can't wait to burp," Jo spoke loudly enough for the barmaid to hear.

The woman belted out a throaty laugh. "What a delightful little boy. He reminds me of my grandson."

Jo beamed.

"Please open the door for me, Jo," Cherry said.

"Sunbeam, I'll carry the drinks," Martinos took delight in Cherry's blush at his words and made a mental note to be more affectionate with her. Funny, but any woman who'd taken a liking

144

to him had been short term. With Cherry, it was different even though he'd eventually leave.

Martinos carried the tray of drinks outside to the spot where Cherry and Jo had claimed a shady table.

"We'll come back here for dinner one night," Cherry said. "The local fish is delicious from what I hear."

"I like fish and chips," Jo shouted.

"You don't need to talk extra loud every time," Martinos said. "Sometimes boys have secrets they whisper to each other." He recalled his friends whispering with Nan the night they had accused him of rape. Stupidly, it hadn't occurred to him to wonder why or suspect skullduggery. He'd paid for that piece of idiocy.

"Oh!" Jo said. "I didn't know that. The boys in my class shout a lot."

"Not when they're planning to cut off your ponytail," Cherry pointed out. "I bet they whisper to each other then."

Jo frowned and picked up her drink. "I guess they talk in whispers sometimes. I haven't seen them do that."

"How is the beer?" Cherry asked.

"It's different from our beer at home," he said. "This is lighter and colder."

"You can try a pint of bitter next time. That's probably more what you're used to," Cherry said.

Another group entered the beer garden with their drinks in hand. The three men glanced in their direction, and Martinos tensed until they moved on and settled at a table on the far side of the garden. Cherry wrapped her hand around his wrist, staying him when the tension within him prompted him to rise.

"It's okay. They're local workers. Fishermen. They're not dangerous to us, merely curious because we're strangers. Most visitors only stay on the island for a few hours."

Martinos forced the rigidity from his muscles and lifted his glass to take a drink. The crisp taste of hops danced across his palate, and the chilly liquid tickled his throat as he swallowed a gulp. The food and beverages here were different but delicious.

Without warning, Jo let out an enormous burp. She slapped her hand to her mouth and stared at them with wide eyes.

"That was a terrific burp," Cherry said, her eyes dancing with humor. "But you need to pardon yourself when you're in a public place. When you're at home with us too."

Martinos winked at Jo. "I'd be proud of that one."

"Pardon me," Joanna whispered.

"Good boy," Cherry said. "We'll walk home once you've finished your drinks."

"What's for dinner?" Joanna asked.

"I might cook a roast chicken."

"Yum," Joanna said. "Can we look in the shop windows before we walk home?"

"That's a girl thing," Cherry reminded her. "But we can pretend it's for my benefit."

"I'd enjoy seeing the products available here," Martinos said. "The shops in the town on the mainland contained so many curious things."

"Yay! You can stop to look, and I'll pretend not to," Joanna whispered.

Martinos shared a grin with Cherry, the strange warmth in his chest not unwelcome.

"Let's go," Cherry said. "Jo, carry your glass back inside to help the barmaid."

"Okay," Jo said.

The suggestion surprised Martinos, but he took possession of Cherry's glass and his, carrying them into the pub.

"Put them on the bar," Cherry said. "When I was at university, I worked in a pub to earn extra money. Bar staff work hard and for long hours. It helps them if we return our dirty glasses."

Something else that had never occurred to Martinos. Another shred of shame filled him, and he promised himself yet again to consider other people with his actions. He'd come to realize small kindnesses meant a lot, and they cost nothing but time.

He opened the door for Cherry and Jo, Cherry's smile of thanks burning off his discomfort at his past actions. While Nan and his ex-friends might call the act weak, he knew better now.

"We'll walk up this way, cross the road, and walk along that side. Is that a plan?" Cherry asked Joanna.

Joanna sent Cherry an exaggerated wink, her entire face

screwing up during the action. "I hate shopping."

"Too bad," Cherry said, her lips quivering with humor. "Move it, young man."

Martinos took Cherry's arm, his skin prickling at the casual contact. The threesome ambled along the rest of the street, pausing now and then to study brightly colored postcards and a sweet shop.

"Can you tell me what these things are in this window?" Martinos asked in a low voice, his attention caught by the contents.

"It's the National Trust shop, and they are a group that helps to preserve old buildings such as castles and houses. That's a china afternoon tea setting, packets of English Breakfast and Earl Grey teas, boxes of oatcakes and shortbread, and jars of strawberry preserves. Their products are fabulous," Cherry said. "I enjoy the books they publish about the buildings, costumes, and food of the era."

"Can we visit this shop when it's open?" Joanna whispered. "I can see books and boy-hats."

"We'll visit on another day." Cherry urged them onward.

As they turned into the wind, a gust seized Cherry's hat. It ripped off her head and fluttered along the footpath before Cherry could slap her hand over the floppy brim.

"I'll get it," Joanna cried and bolted after the runaway hat.

"Watch for traffic," Cherry warned, seconds before Joanna stepped onto the road and ran across the street.

A man walking on the other side of the road grasped the bright pink hat before Joanna got to it. Martinos froze. He knew that man, and he didn't want him anywhere near Cherry or Joanna.

Nemyr, The Scary, was not the dragon one wanted near his family.

Instinctively, Martinos reached for his dragon, determined to protect his woman. Of course, nothing happened, his dragon suppressed by the magic of the armband. He pushed harder, and a sharp pain speared through his head.

Helpless against his former friend, Martinos struggled as Nemyr eyed Cherry like a juicy morsel.

By Lodar, if Nemyr recognized him, they'd be in trouble.

Every muscle in Martinos's body tensed, waiting for Nemyr to explode into his dragon form and incinerate them without a second thought.

Nemyr glanced at Martinos, but the dragon's expression never shifted. His broad, appreciative leer remained as he dismissed Martinos and ogled Cherry again.

"Your hat, my dear," he said, his suggestive voice carrying to Martinos.

His smarmy charm shoved temper into Martinos, yet he hesitated to act on his instinct to punch Nemyr. The last thing they wanted was to draw attention to themselves. Nemyr was here in his human form, and Martinos presumed he wished to travel incognito. Martinos strolled closer, every sense on high alert.

Cherry accepted her hat from the dragon. "Thank you."

"You shouldn't hide your pretty red hair beneath that pink monstrosity," Nemyr drawled. "It's a crime against your beauty."

"Cherry. Jo," Martinos said in a harsh voice. "It's time to go home."

He grasped Cherry's arm and gave Jo a gentle nudge away from Nemyr.

Cherry sent him a puzzled glance but thankfully didn't ask questions or take him to task for his rudeness. He didn't relax until they were a hundred meters away from Nemyr. He risked a glance over his shoulder and found Leo's brother was still staring at Cherry. He hadn't recognized Martinos despite their past friendship.

Aware this was a piece of luck, Martinos hustled Cherry and Jo farther away, widening the distance between them and Nemyr.

"What's wrong?" Cherry asked.

Martinos didn't reply until he could no longer see Nemyr. What the hell was the dragon doing here? How had he passed through the barrier?

"Martinos," Cherry spoke sharply, her tone demanding an answer.

"That was one of my former friends. Nemyr, The Scary."

Cherry halted abruptly. "A dragon?"

"Yes."

"Why didn't you ask him how he got here?"

"Former friend," Martinos repeated. "He's dangerous. His title is The Scary because of his brutality and his enjoyment in hurting others. He helped my sister Nan set me up for the rape charges. He's part of the reason I ended up in the dungeon."

"He didn't seem concerned at his presence on this side of the barrier," Cherry said. "He was charming."

"Stay away from him," Martinos barked. "He's a heartless dragon and cares nothing for others. I hated the way he looked at you."

Cherry frowned. "How did he look at me?"

"Like you were a sweet treat for his consumption," Martinos said.

"Are we in danger?"

"We might be if he recognized me."

"Is he following us?"

Martinos scanned the area behind him. He didn't sense Nemyr following them, but his instincts were no longer as sharp with his dragon bound.

Cherry's forehead creased in a frown. "Jo, don't get too far ahead of us, please."

Martinos glanced over his shoulder again. He didn't glimpse Nemyr, but unease still sat on Martinos's shoulders.

Questions filled him. Nemyr was here on Holy Island. Why? What was his purpose? "Did Rena say when the druid might arrive?"

"No. We should keep exploring the island and hope we run into him or find a way to help you."

"Now that Nemyr is here, it's dangerous to wander the island."

"You think we should stay in the cottage?"

Martinos ran a hand through his hair, frustration riding him. "I want to get the armband removed to break the spell binding my dragon, but the truth is my dragon might be past help."

"He might be dead?"

Martinos screwed his eyes shut for a moment, not wanting to face this prospect. "I hope not. It's a possibility, though."

"What will you do?"

"I don't know." Frustration shimmered in him. Indecision.

"You could always ask this Nemyr what he's doing here."

"No. Too dangerous since he has his full powers. There is nothing to stop him from killing me and stealing you away. Believe me, he's capable of much worse. The dragon has no conscience. Jo might get hurt."

Cherry grasped his hand and fell into step with him. "We must take care not to run into him again then. I still think we should continue exploring. Why didn't he recognize you?"

"I wore my hair cut very short and was clean-shaven. My clothes were regal and expensive. I've lost weight and no longer resemble a spoiled, pampered aristocrat. I wasn't a nice dragon then. Normally, my scent would've given me away, but the armband took care of that danger since it's suppressing my dragon."

"You've changed that much?"

"I've mentioned before I had lots of time to reflect on my past. Leo's generosity in freeing me and Gwenyth's kindness gave me an extra incentive to change. When I promised to repay them for releasing me, Gwenyth told me I should pay it forward. I'd never heard of that before, but I understand what she meant now."

"That's the sort of thing Liza would've said. Despite Tony causing so many problems for her, she was still open-hearted and generous."

Sadness filled her, and Martinos gave her a brief hug.

"I'm unsure of what to do for the best," Martinos confessed.

Cherry cocked her head, her brow furrowed. "Is it possible that this Nemyr is just visiting Holy Island? That dragons have the ability or the means to travel between our worlds?"

"I don't know," Martinos said. "I presume druids can move between the worlds."

"All right. How about this? What if dragons come here to get things they can't obtain on any of your islands? Maybe technology or other items that are rare in your world. They might even travel here to party or to meet women. There could be many reasons someone might wish to travel."

Martinos nodded. "I suppose that is possible. If Nemyr and his brothers bribed a druid in charge of the magic, they might travel without obstacles."

"Blackmail? Is that possible?"

"I suppose."

"How do we find out? I mean, if that's the case, there must be a portal between the worlds."

Martinos pondered the subject, unease filling him as the only answer presented itself. "If we see Nemyr or anyone else I recognize, I'll follow them."

"Won't they sense you?"

Martinos's mouth twisted at the irony. "Normally, but because the druids bound my dragon and my T-shirt covered my armband, Nemyr suspected nothing." A snort escaped him. "He was more interested in ogling you."

"I'll wear a different hat next time."

Martinos nodded while praying there wouldn't be a next time. If he spotted another dragon, he'd hustle Cherry out of sight.

No way did he intend to place her or Jo in danger again.

CHAPTER 10

Hard Chest. Warm Arms.
Sexy Times

Martinos was quiet after they arrived back at the cottage. While she prepared the chicken for the oven, Martinos showed Joanna how to draw a dragon. Once Joanna was busy sketching dragons of her own, Martinos came to help Cherry. She set him to work peeling potatoes while marveling at the arresting man with his strong body, his long black hair currently loose, and the sexy beard that hugged his jawline. It was an inspiring, heart-pounding sight and contentment pulsed through her.

"I enjoy preparing food," he confessed, breaking the silence. "In the past, I never considered how the food appeared on the table.

The servants produced meals when I summoned them."

"You clicked your fingers, and food materialized?"

"Pretty much. I find it satisfying to contribute toward our meals."

"Some men consider cooking women's work," Cherry said, pulling a face.

"But we watched a cooking show last night. A man showed us how to make a pie."

"Yes, we have male chefs, but a few men cling to the past and traditional roles. For example, my friend Liza—her ex-husband expected her to have the evening meal on the table when he arrived home from work or from drinking with his friends. If Liza didn't have the meal ready on time, he'd shout at her. Sometimes, if he'd been drinking, he'd hit her."

"I dislike this man."

"What do the male dragons do in your world?"

"Touché," Martinos said. "We have servants who are disciplined if our meals do not arrive on time. Now that I understand it takes time to prepare, I won't act with such haste or inconsideration."

"What happens when the servants don't move fast enough?"

"They lose their jobs," Martinos said. "In a bygone age, they might've lost their lives."

"A similar dynamic then. Someone in power punishes those in a weaker position."

"Yes." Martinos frowned. "I have many apologies and

transgressions to rectify."

"Did you dismiss a servant?"

"No. My mother or sister took charge of the interior duties. At least I assume they did because the servants changed with regularity." He paused.

"What?"

"I hate to admit this, but if a servant girl grabbed my attention, I did my best to seduce her and thought nothing of it. None of the servants had the power to say no to me."

"We have laws against that here. The courts can send culprits to jail or enforce large fines. That's how seriously we take the matter. Everyone has the right to say no."

"No one worries in the Dragon Isles. Servants have no rights. I'm ashamed," he murmured, and Cherry could tell he truly meant his words. "In the past, it never bothered me. You and Gwenyth have opened my eyes and my mind to different thinking."

"Your world sounds terrifying. It must be a daunting world for those without power."

"Yes," Martinos said, his frown etching into his forehead. "I can see that. The thing is our world has been this way ever since the druids created the barrier. Earlier, in fact. The barrier kept us safe from humans who wished to kill us, and we continued with our usual behavior."

Cherry hated to think of him using servants in that manner, although he received points for understanding right and wrong and the fact his past behavior bothered him. "Promise me you will never repeat your behavior, and I'll continue to speak to you instead of giving you the cold shoulder."

"I don't know what a cold shoulder is, but I hope to make changes within my district. My sister...I shudder to imagine her actions with no one to hold her in check. Hopefully, my parents have limited her power. She can be cruel, and she isn't trustworthy. I've learned that to my cost."

"Let's change the subject. I'll call Rena after dinner. If her luck holds, and she can avoid Tony, she'll cross to the island this week. Meantime, I vote to continue our explorations. We'll go on walks, check out the beach again, visit the castle, and go into town for dinner one night. If we spot any dragons, we'll walk in the opposite direction."

Martinos turned to her then and cupped her face in his big hands. "Seriously, we must take care. Any dragon on Holy Island is dangerous to us. To you and Joanna."

"We will proceed with caution. I promise, but we can't barricade ourselves inside the cottage either. Jo, for one, will become grumpy, and I want to explore. Any dragons visiting the town will try to blend in with the humans. Won't they?"

"We must pray that is so." Martinos released her and picked up the final potato to peel. Once he'd done that, he tidied the work surface. "What next?" he asked in eager expectation.

Warmth filled Cherry at Martinos's enthusiasm to embrace her life and the everyday tasks she threw his way. The man, this dragon, filled her with hope for the future. Their future. Except, he wanted to return to his home while she had her bookstore, her life here. She had Joanna to protect. One day at a time, she cautioned herself. No use borrowing more trouble. One day at a time was the way to proceed.

She pressed a button on the oven to check the timer. "We wait for the chicken and potatoes to cook. Once that's done, we can make the gravy. We'll have peas and carrots, but they're frozen, so we'll cook them last. Let's sit outside with a glass of wine."

When he nodded his agreement, she pulled two wineglasses from the cupboard.

Martinos collected the wine from the fridge without her asking. He didn't give himself enough credit. The dragon-man had acted the gentleman from the moment she and Joanna had discovered him on the beach.

"Joanna, we'll be sitting outside on the deck."

"Yes, Aunt Cherry. Do you like my dragons?" Joanna shoved her sketchbook at Cherry, the pages a profusion of color. She'd drawn a flight of dragons, coloring the beasts in distinct colors.

"Do dragons come in red and green?" she asked.

"Uncle Martinos told me they did," Joanna said.

Cherry nodded. "Okay. Shout if you need us."

Martinos poured the wine after retrieving the glasses from her. He pulled out a seat for her and waited in expectation.

Cherry dropped onto the seat and beamed at him. Delight—a pleased-with-himself satisfaction—danced in his expression as he completed the gentlemanly act he'd picked up from watching a movie with her. She was right. He *could* fit in with this world. "Joanna mentioned you told her dragons are born in a variety of colors."

"Yes," Martinos murmured. "I'm a red dragon. My parents are both red. Nan is a black dragon which is rarer. Other dragons are blue or green. Red, blue, and green are the predominant colors, but occasionally, a bronze dragon will show up in a family."

"Interesting. I thought the idea of colorful dragons came from cartoons."

Martinos chuckled. "You've learned new facts."

Instead of remaining seated, Cherry gathered her bravery and plopped herself on Martinos's lap. To her relief, he hummed in approval and drew her close.

"Don't worry," Cherry whispered. "We'll work out a way for you to go back."

"What I might find on my return worries me," Martinos said.

"Will your sister fight you for control?"

"Yes. One of us will die."

"No!" Cherry said. "What about your parents?"

"Please don't worry. This is our way when there is conflict," Martinos murmured, his arms tightening. "My parents... I haven't heard from them since my arrest." He pressed an open-mouthed kiss to her neck, and her breath caught. One big hand cupped her jaw, gently turning her face toward him.

Seconds later, his mouth covered hers. Their previous kisses had been tentative. This one held authority. Passion. And it stole her breath.

A moan of pleasure escaped her as she gripped Martinos's shoulders and held tight. Their tongues tangled. Her heart beat faster, and her world narrowed to their kiss.

"Why are you kissing Uncle Martinos?" Joanna asked from right beside them.

Cherry jumped, and Martinos let out a strangled *oomph*. Heat invaded her cheeks, and she cursed her propensity to blush, but it wasn't every day she sat on a man's erection. Times, they were changing.

"Uncle Martinos?"

"Your Aunt Cherry and I like each other," Martinos said in a husky voice.

"Oh," Joanna said. "Okay. I like both of you." She came closer and kissed Cherry on the cheek. She repeated the move with Martinos then wandered away without another comment.

Martinos spluttered out a laugh, and Cherry giggled.

"Next time, we'll find a private place to kiss," Martinos said.

The banked lust in his eyes had Cherry breathing faster, harder. "Next time?"

"I want you, Cherry. I want to skim my hands over your

gorgeous curves again. This time, I'd prefer to see them. Taste you. All of you."

"Oh," Cherry whispered.

"Don't you want the same thing?"

"Yes," she agreed without hesitation. While she wasn't a woman who jumped into an affair, it was different with Martinos. They'd spent hours talking and learning about each other. She felt as if she understood him, both the good and the bad.

"Tonight," Martinos promised.

"Tonight," she agreed, and they sealed the deal with a kiss.

After dinner, they relaxed on the deck again. Even when Joanna went to bed, Martinos didn't hustle her. She appreciated his lack of haste, and it reconfirmed her decision. No doubt, if she were with her friends, she'd have discussed the pros and cons to death. Liza would've cautioned her while Rena would've voted hell, yeah. Go for it.

Cherry smiled. Martinos might think he was the one who was transforming, but she was making changes too. She trusted herself to make the right decision, her confidence growing in bounds.

"I enjoy sitting out here at the day's end," Martinos said. "The stars are so bright. I've never taken the time to watch them before or to listen to the night sounds."

Almost on cue, an owl hooted from a nearby tree.

"What animals do you have on your islands?" Cherry asked.

"We have lots of birds: owls, birds of the forest, and seabirds. We have wolves, although my people have hunted them to extinction on Smoking Isle. Let me see—squirrels, badgers. Otters. We also have a nocturnal wild cat. They've become rare as have the badgers. During the last volcano eruption, the lava flow destroyed a vast tract of forest. Many small animals and birds perished."

"It sounds as if your animals and birds are similar to ours. Despite our conservation efforts, many of our animals are extinct, too, or at least endangered. We no longer have wolves. Men hunted them to extinction around one hundred years ago. Are your plants similar?"

"From what I've seen. Why don't you come here? That way I can kiss you while enjoying the night."

Cherry closed the gap willingly, her body coming alive the second Martinos's arms curled around her. His presence made her feel safe. Happy. Confident.

"I tried to ring Rena, but she didn't answer. In the end, I sent her a text asking when she'd arrive. She has the address. It wouldn't surprise me if she turned up without warning."

"Then we shouldn't waste time," Martinos said, a naughty twinkle noticeable even in the dim light. He kissed her slowly, deeply, the passion igniting between them.

Martinos pulled away a fraction, his breath warm on her cheek. "Suddenly, I'm feeling tired and need to lie down." He helped her to her feet, a cheeky grin curving his lips. "Will you lie with me?"

"Yes."

Martinos picked up their empty glasses and clasped her hand with his free one. "Let's go."

After locking the cottage, Martinos guided her along the passage.

"The bed in my room is bigger," she said.

"Lead the way."

Cherry released his hand and pushed open the door to her bedroom. Part of her had wondered if she'd second-guess her decision, but not one protest reared its ugly head. The click of the closing door had her pulse racing. Not in fear but in anticipation.

"Can I take off your T-shirt? I've wanted to get my hands on your chest ever since I first saw you on the beach."

Martinos placed his hands at his sides while she lifted the T-shirt to reveal his abs and tattoo. He leaned forward to aid her due to their height difference.

Cherry switched on one of the bedside lamps even though she preferred to hide in darkness. Martinos didn't bring out her self-consciousness. Each of his actions bolstered her confidence, and she loved this about him.

"You've gained a little weight," she said after doing a quick survey of his chest.

His dragon still curled low on his belly, the creature's despondency and dejection palpable from its slump. She bit her lip and slid her gaze to the wide band on his left biceps. The armband held decorative spirals and knots, similar to those she'd seen in

Celtic knotwork. From memory, these shapes were continuous with no beginning and no ending and represented eternity. Did that mean the armband was unbreakable?

"It's the delicious food," Martinos said, his eyes darkening when he saw the drift of her gaze. "When I was younger, I refused to eat anything except meat. Poor people ate vegetables. Humans ate vegetables."

"You've changed. Stop comparing yourself with then and now. Some people have rougher childhoods, while others aren't taught right from wrong. Children might miss the lesson of values because the family units break down for one reason or another. It's who you become when you're an adult that matters. You've changed, Martinos. You shouldn't keep telling me what a horrid dragon you are when I see an adult trying to improve—to be the best they can. It's your journey that matters."

"You make it sound so simple," he murmured, his expression dark and stony.

"For you, it is easy. Keep doing what you're doing. You think of other people whenever you act. I've seen you do this instinctively with Joanna, and with me when we're interacting with other people. You want to improve, and you have."

This conversation was a revelation to her. Each of them lacked confidence in their own way, for different reasons, but together they could become unstoppable. A sharp pang of loss swept her before she could recall the traitorous emotion and the feelings that came with the sentiment. With Martinos, she had no rights. He'd never made promises, nor did she expect them given their circumstances. But this—she wanted his body and his focus with her every particle.

Regrets.

She'd worry later once he'd left her to return to his world. Her gaze landed on his chest and his dejected red dragon, and this time, she gave into temptation. She reached out, pressed her fingertips to his pectoral muscles. He gasped, or she did. Both of them, perhaps.

His skin blazed beneath her touch. "Are you hot because you're a dragon?"

The corners of his eyes crinkled in amusement. "It's you," he confessed, his voice husky. "You heat me."

"Rubbish," she muttered. "I've never done that to any male."

"I'm not any male." He captured one of her hands and lifted it to his mouth. His warm lips surrounded a digit, and Cherry swore he'd created a path directly to her sex. Her pulse banged into a fight-or-flight sprint, yet her feet were frozen to the spot. Their gazes met, and for an instant, she'd swear she glimpsed something else in his irises.

She blinked, and when she met his eyes again, they were full of sensual male regard. Heat. Desire.

She gasped as his tongue swept over her finger, the blast of carnal energy zapping her sex yet again. Her ex-boyfriend had always told her she took forever to warm up for the sexual act. He couldn't be bothered in the end.

Martinos bit down on her finger, the tiny jolt of pain swinging her gaze back to his face. This time, he wore a frown.

"Where did your mind go?"

"I...I..." She trailed off, shaking her head at her inability to speak.

"I want your sexy mind here with me. Has anyone ever spanked you?"

She shuddered. "Yes. I hated it."

"The perfect punishment for letting your mind wander. Eyes front." He bit her finger again to ensure she understood his words were no mere threat.

"I'm surprised you want me," she confessed.

"We've had this discussion."

"Um, yes."

"Then know if I weren't wildly attracted to you, I would've thanked you for dinner and your company and gone to my room. On my own. I didn't do that."

"Ah. No?"

He released her finger with a pop and grasped her shoulders. "I'm here because I find you attractive and desirable. You intrigue me in a way I've never discovered with another woman." He ran his fingers along her arm, over her T-shirt sleeve, tickling her bare skin until he reached her fingertips. His touch left a raft of goosebumps in its wake. Martinos curled their fingers together and placed her hand on the bulge between his thighs.

"This is not disinterest. I am interested in exploring your generous curves until you scream your pleasure."

"Um, what if we wake Joanna?"

"She won't hear because you'll be screaming into my mouth."

"Oh. Thank you. Acceptable plan."

His chuckle held passion along with humor. "That is excellent. Shall we get started?"

"Yes, please."

"So polite."

"I'm nervous. A giveaway. I'm always extra polite when anxiety gets to me."

"I see. In that case, it'd be best for me to take over this first time. I'll whisper dirty sweet nothings into your ear to let you know what I intend to do with your delectable body. And I promise to keep your mind so busy you won't have time to worry or compare me with past lovers."

"There haven't been many." She'd hate it if her lack of experience caused him disappointment.

"That is excellent. I find myself excited to teach you. Let's begin. I will sit on the side of the bed while you take off each item of your clothing for me."

"I'm terrible at stripping." She gulped on recalling another failed seduction that she'd attempted when she'd felt her ex-boyfriend drifting away. She'd wanted to spice up their love life. Oh, she'd entertained him all right. He'd laughed at her awkward attempt to initiate their lovemaking.

"Let me be the judge of that." He sat, his legs spread, the bulge of his cock on display while the bare skin of his shoulders glinted in the light.

Cherry imagined Rena urging her onward. She sensed that once her friends got to know him, they'd approve of Martinos, so she swallowed her unease and wholeheartedly embraced this seduction.

She removed her sandals first. Lesson learned from her first seduction effort many months ago. *Take that!* Cherry hummed under her breath and swiveled her hips. A growl escaped Martinos and encouraged, she peeled off her leggings and kicked them into the corner of the bedroom. Still humming, she lifted the hem of her tunic and even managed a wink before she whisked it over her head and tossed that in the corner too.

Now dressed only in her bra and panties—thankfully a matching smoky-gray pair—she rocked her hips again, her gaze intent on Martinos. His gaze blazed with approval, which fed her confidence. She reached behind her back to flick open her bra and leaned forward a fraction to tease him with glimpses of her flesh.

"More," he whispered.

Cherry allowed her bra straps to slip down her arms before turning to wriggle her scantily clad backside in his direction.

A deep growl had her turning in surprise. Lust shone on his face, and she dropped her arms, releasing her bra.

"Come here," he ordered.

She scurried to his side without hesitation, only releasing a small *eep* of shock when he swept her off her feet and planted her on his knee. His eyes traveled to her generous breasts. Her taut nipples. Martinos dipped his head and took one pouting peak into his mouth. His wet heat surrounded her, and when he drew on her tip, she moaned. His hands turned greedy, and he cupped and shaped her flesh while his mouth drove her crazy with a combo of nips and sucks.

Cherry gripped his head. "Martinos, please. More." She'd never realized how arousing it might be when a man paid such exquisite attention to her boobs. "So good," she breathed as his pinching fingers shot pain/pleasure surging to the spot between her thighs. The ache in her sex increased, and she squirmed on his lap.

"Martinos!"

"Shush, sunbeam. Let me explore your gorgeous body. I've imagined the fit of your tits in my hands since we met. They are perfection. Full and luscious and responsive. I wonder if I can get you off just by playing with these beauties?"

No! She didn't want that right now. "Maybe another time," she blurted. "I ache." She squirmed on his lap, seeking a spot to rub her aching flesh against to assuage the tension sweeping her.

Martinos gripped her hip with one hard hand. He pinched her nipple while sealing her shocked gasp with his mouth. She relaxed against his hard chest. "Obedient girl." He swept a hand over her back until he came to her butt.

The heat from his hand radiated through her skimpy panties, and she sucked in an excited breath. With ease, he stood, holding her in his arms without a single grunt.

"I crave a taste of your sweetness," he whispered, and his tone was more a sensual purr.

Cherry nodded assent, her stomach twisting with nerves and excitement. This, she had never experienced before since her ex hadn't enjoyed her taste. She grinned. No more thoughts or comparisons with Mr. Ex. The guy was a dick. Both Liza and Rena had assured her this was so after they'd coaxed the tale from her.

Martinos placed her on the bed and peeled off her panties before she had even settled. Cool air sizzled against her hot flesh when he parted her legs. He ran his tongue from the inside of her knee to her inner thigh before licking her center.

"Oh! Yes," she whispered, a quivering mess of anticipation. "If you dare stop, I'll wrestle you to the ground."

He laughed, his amusement a warm puff of air against her clit. "*Mmm,*" he hummed as he introduced a finger. He traced the petals of her sex, parting her folds in a way that plain thrilled her. He licked a delicate path along her seam, stopping millimeters from her swollen nub. She jerked her hips, seeking more pressure.

"Tell me what you want," he murmured in a seductive voice.

"Pressure," she wailed. "I need more of your touch. Your fingers and mouth."

He gave her both, not seeming to mind the wetness of her arousal, her smell or taste. The knot of her sex throbbed and ached, each of his touches ratcheting up the tension in her lower belly.

"Let go, sunbeam. Come for me. Can you do that?"

"I want to. I'm trying."

Martinos's lips shaped her clit and tugged with a light touch. Her entire body jerked. Shuddered. For an instant, she experienced an out-of-body sensation as if she were flying before she sprang back into sharp focus with explosive pleasure. She gasped as Martinos stroked her with the gentlest of touches. Her sex clenched around his finger, gripping it tightly as she climaxed.

"That's my girl," he murmured. "You came so beautifully for me. Such an honor to watch."

A blush suffused her cheeks on hearing his praise. He gave her nub a languorous lick, kicking off a quick series of spasms.

"You have more for me," he said. "I can't wait to sink into that juicy pussy of yours. You'll soak my dick in your arousal and I'll come inside you."

"I don't have any condoms, but I am on birth control," Cherry said.

The practicalities brought another surge of heat to her face, and not for the first time, she wished she'd quit doing that. A twenty-four-year-old woman shouldn't still blush like a champion. "I mean, I'm not sure if dragons and humans can have offspring. What I'm saying is I'm safe. Don't worry. *Gah*, Cherry! Shut up already." She pressed her lips together to prevent more words from spilling forth. It seemed men-induced orgasms made her loopy. Who knew?

"Stop," he whispered and kissed her to enforce his order. When she calmed and started kissing him back, he lifted his head. "You're right to ask. Yes, we can have offspring together. This is the first time I have been with a woman since I escaped from the dungeon. I carry no pox or any other diseases."

"I'm still on birth control. That's something we use to stop the formation of a child."

Martinos issued a hearty sigh. "You cannot understand how thrilled and excited I am to hear this because, in my world, there is always a risk of pregnancy. Although I am certain I'd enjoy your mouth on my cock, I'm craving the tightness of your pussy."

"Martinos." Everything inside Cherry fluttered.

Without taking his gaze from her, Martinos levered off the bed and yanked at his trousers. He wore nothing beneath, and his erection spilled free, the crown shiny with pre-cum. Fierceness etched into his features as he prowled back and dropped on the mattress to join her. He gazed at her for a long moment before his focus drifted down her body and back.

Never had she felt more beautiful. Desirable.

Martinos pushed the experiences through her with a one-two punch of awareness. At that moment, she understood, she'd been chasing the wrong men, trying to fit in rather than finding one suitable for her.

Martinos fit like a snug puzzle piece.

Their lips met, gentle at first until passion spilled over, dragging them over to a place where sensation and togetherness ruled. Martinos parted her legs with one muscular thigh. He nuzzled her breasts, gave her a hint of pain, having already learned what she enjoyed. He surged over her body, weighing her down in a way that should have overwhelmed her. Instead, she loved the downward pressure of his body and the way he caged her in his strength.

Martinos reached between them and dragged the head of his shaft along her seam. This time, he groaned in concert with her.

"Martinos, please." She hated to wait any longer. Greedily, she wanted to grab and experience more of that delirious pleasure.

Martinos brushed the wild red curls away from her face and smiled as he positioned himself at her entrance. Cherry tensed at the fullness, but Martinos slowed. He distracted her by playing with her breasts and sucking on her nipples while he tunneled inside her. The temptation to touch and participate grew, and she gave in, running her hands over his muscular back.

"You look so much better after a few days of rest and decent food."

"I feel better." He grinned at her. "Especially right now." He drew back a fraction and pushed deep again. "What do you need to come again?" he asked. "Once I start, I won't have much control because it has been a long time for me."

"Don't worry about me."

"I will," he countered, his voice stern. He pulled back and thrust, using a grinding action that hit her in precisely the right spot.

"Yes," she murmured, her eyelashes fluttering.

"If I lose my sense of rhythm, I want you to touch yourself. Take what you need. Please. There's nothing better than your body clenching mine. The tiny spasms of your pleasure will take my enjoyment to an extra level." He shook her gently in emphasis. "Do you hear me?"

"Yes, Martinos." Cherry suited the action to words and squirmed her hand between their straining bodies. She groaned when her finger brushed her sensitive flesh.

Martinos upped the pace of his thrusts, his hips snapping in jerky movements while his breathing grew hoarse. Cherry held him, fascinated by the raw passion on his face. She stroked her clit, groaning when the root of Martinos's cock hit her at the perfect angle.

His next hard thrust sent her into a spiral of pleasure, and she cried out, her body awash with exquisite sensation. She gripped Martinos tightly, glorying in the aftershocks. Martinos groaned, plunged deep, and remained embedded in her flesh, his cock pulsing in hard, rhythmic spurts. He relaxed his tense muscles and sought her mouth without opening his eyes.

"Are we still alive?" he asked in a deep voice once he'd parted their lips. "I can't ever remember sex feeling that satisfying." He withdrew a fraction, and Cherry made a sound of protest. She enjoyed feeling him inside and out, and he was right. Sex had never thrilled her in that manner.

Martinos woke the next morning with a naked Cherry wrapped within his arms. By Lodar, she was beautiful. Every part of her appealed to him. Her body. Her mind. Her character. He kissed her brow, and she murmured sleepily.

Martinos listened for Joanna and heard nothing. Still early, which gave him time to love Cherry again, savor her gorgeous curves and experience them wrapped around his dick.

He fitted his lips to hers while he cupped a heavy breast. Now that he had slightly more control, he couldn't wait to mount her from behind and run his hands over her soft, full buttocks.

He sensed the moment she came awake and started participating in this loving.

"Are you sore?" He hadn't held back at the end there, his urgency making him rougher than he should've been.

"Not really."

"We don't have to have sex again this morning."

"Never say you're going to leave me hanging after kissing me awake," she said, her smile teasing and bright.

He curled away from her, lifting her into the position he wanted.

"Hey," she protested. "I've told you this isn't my favorite body part."

"And I've told you you're wrong," he countered. "Let me show you."

"If you're positive." She agreed to his urging, but it was clear she still held her doubt close.

Martinos forced her upright on her hands and knees, his fingers firm on her body. He licked across one soft, cushiony buttock and gave her a hint of his teeth.

"Ow." She turned her head in a glance of censure.

"Just making sure you're paying attention. I want you to understand every part of you is beautiful to me. Besides, in this position, I can play with your breasts or your clit as I see fit."

"Yes, Martinos." Although the words were meek, her attitude reeked of stroppy.

He grinned and entertained himself by exploring her back. She bore freckles on her skin, and he licked over them. One of his hands crept down to play with a breast. Her creamy flesh overflowed his hand. It fascinated him. Thrilled him. The ache in his balls had him hastening his explorations. He ran a finger between her buttocks, grinning at her start. Then he hit her clit, and she softened beneath him.

"I ache to see my cock disappearing into your pussy," he murmured. "But first, I need to get you nice and wet for me."

"I'm wet," she protested.

He squeezed a nipple to give her a hint of pain. She rewarded him with a groan, so he repeated the move. "You'd enjoy me spanking you."

"No. No, I wouldn't," Cherry said quickly.

"Savoring pain with your loving is not a cause for shame. I want you to have maximum enjoyment from our time together. Nothing is out of bounds if we both relish the process." He tightened his grip on her nipple and wished he had his old collection of toys with him because he sensed Cherry might appreciate having her boundaries tested.

Martinos spent time readying her body for him again. The urge for speed grabbed at his balls. His cock swelled and his pre-cum leaked from his tip. They'd made love a second time during the darkness of the night before falling asleep. Twice wasn't enough to sate him. Greedily, he wished they could stay in bed for the entire day, but they needed to recommence their search for a way for him to leave the island.

Then there was Joanna.

Martinos teased more arousal from Cherry before tucking himself at her entrance and slipping into her liquid heat. He took his time, pushing to the root and holding steady while her flesh trembled around his cock. He played with her breasts, having learned how sensitive they were and lazily thrust and withdrew, gliding and stroking in a manner that pushed their satisfaction to new heights. Cherry trembled beneath him.

"Touch yourself," he whispered against her ear. "Touch my cock too. Tease us both while I amuse myself with your breasts."

She balanced herself on her knees and one hand, and seconds later, she stroked her clit. She touched his shaft, the delicate caress sending an extra burst of pleasure along his dick.

"Perfect," Martinos crooned. He kept up the steady surge and retreat, his hips moving faster and faster. "Cherry, sunbeam. Are you ready to come?"

"Close," she whispered.

For the first time in his memory, Martinos lost control. He thrust hard, his climax tingling to life and rolling toward completion with the speed of a furious dragon on the hunt. Cherry's smaller hand rubbed the base of his shaft. A loud moan pushed up his throat, his orgasm ripping from his balls and bursting from his cock.

It took long moments for him to come back to himself, a long moment for him to understand that Cherry hadn't joined him in the free fall of lust.

"Sunbeam," he whispered.

He pulled back, separating their bodies. With gentle hands, he turned Cherry and splayed her thighs.

"What...?"

"Let me help you," he said, and he dipped his head to lick her slit. He tasted himself. He tasted Cherry. Her hips lifted into his mouth, and she shuddered, a low moan of delight spilling from her lips.

"Martinos. Oh, my goodness. That is... That is fantastic." She cried out, the tiny nub giving a series of spasms beneath his mouth. She sighed, the tension dispersing from her body. Her gaze met his. "Thank you."

He sprawled on the bed beside her and sought her kiss. "It was entirely my pleasure."

They wrapped their arms around each other and lay there, savoring their closeness and the sensual delight they'd experienced together.

Cherry drifted back to sleep, but Martinos remained awake as the early morning turned to dawn. He heard footsteps outside the bedroom.

"Aunt Cherry."

Martinos whisked the covers over their bodies as the door creaked open.

Joanna came to a halt, her brown eyes widening. "Uncle Martinos."

Martinos placed his finger to his lips. "Shh. Aunt Cherry is still asleep."

"Is she tired?"

"Yes," Martinos said, his lips quivering with satisfaction since he was the reason for Cherry's fatigue. "Can you dress yourself?"

"Yes," Joanna said.

"You get dressed, and I'll do the same. We'll make Aunt Cherry breakfast for a change."

"Yes!" Joanna repeated with enthusiasm.

Martinos waited for Joanna to leave before he turned to Cherry. "She's gone to her room."

"I'm so embarrassed."

"Why? She didn't appear upset by finding us together."

"I was waiting for questions," Cherry said. "She would've remembered Liza sharing a bed with Tony."

"Sleeping by your side makes me happy. I want to do it again soon."

"I... Maybe," Cherry said.

Martinos climbed out of bed and pulled on his clothes while monitoring the door. He didn't comment on Cherry's reaction but vowed to change her mind. One night was not enough.

Chapter 11

Holy Island Happenings

Cherry kept sneaking glances at Martinos while they ate scrambled eggs and toast, both of which Martinos had cooked. He'd also made a pot of coffee and poured a glass of milk for Joanna. The man was handy. She nibbled her bottom lip and forced herself not to gawk at him again.

She'd acted silly this morning, treating Martinos as if he'd done something wrong. Their lovemaking had involved two people.

On impulse, she reached across the table to take Martinos's hand. "We'll go exploring this morning and keep an eye out for dragons."

Martinos nodded, his expression softening. "Excellent plan."

Cherry's phone rang. "Hello."

"It's me," Rena said. "My dreams were full of trees. All night."

"What sort of trees?"

"Magical ones."

Cherry frowned and wondered if her friend had lost the plot. "Did they resemble normal trees?" she asked, humoring her.

Rena snorted. "They were green."

"That's a great help. Do you think your dream meant something? That it was important?"

There was a lengthy pause where Cherry imagined Rena shrugging. "Who knows? All my dreams are weird."

"I'll tell Martinos," Cherry said, and she would even if the idea of magical trees sounded crazy. She hadn't truly believed she'd meet a man on the beach either, and she'd been wrong about that. "Will you be here soon?"

"Not yet," Rena said. "I'm still in Edinburgh. I'm staying for another day."

"Why? Have you seen Tony?"

"No, but someone broke into my apartment again. I want to use caution. I'd hate to lead Tony straight to you and Joanna."

"All right, although Martinos will keep us safe."

"I thought he'd lost his dragon powers."

"He's not useless," Cherry snapped. "He could handle Tony."

"*Ooh,*" Rena cooed. "You're defensive on his behalf. Sounds serious."

"Sometimes, you're irritating. You concentrate on your dream man and leave me to watch things here."

"Hmm, interesting. I almost wish I was there to scope out the Holy Island happenings."

Cherry sniffed. "Enough. Tony is the villain here, and the one to watch. Pick on Tony, not me."

Rena snorted, the sound between a laugh and a snicker. "Fair enough. Don't forget the tree thing. No idea what it means, but who knows."

The phone clicked on Rena's end, and Cherry placed her mobile on the tabletop. "Rena dreamed of trees last night. Magic ones. Does that spark any thoughts?"

Martinos shook his head. "No."

Cherry shrugged. "Oh, well. Maybe one of us will have a brainwave. Meanwhile, let's go exploring. Joanna, have you finished? Are you ready to go on an adventure?"

"Yay!" Joanna wiped her milk mustache with the back of her hand.

"Go and wash your face and clean your teeth. You start, and I'll be in to help you in a few minutes."

Joanna thumped down the passage, channeling her boy persona again. Chortling, Cherry shook her head and picked up Joanna's empty glass. Martinos helped her clear the dishes and tidy the kitchen.

"We'll take the car today. Maybe drive along the main street in town and check out the shops and visitors. People-watching."

Martinos nodded. "Splendid idea."

Despite looking, neither she nor Martinos spotted Nemyr as they drove through the central part of the town. With a sigh of relief, because the dragon's presence yesterday had scared her, Cherry pulled into the pay and display car park. "We'll explore the castle, but first we have to walk to it. A fifteen-minute walk."

"Where is it?" Joanna called, once again firmly in her boy-disguise.

Cherry pointed at the castle which sat atop a hill. She scanned for trees, but there weren't any in the vicinity. From what she'd seen, Holy Island was flat and treeless. "Let's go."

Cherry grasped Joanna's hand, and their threesome walked through the town, past the harbor. Once they arrived, Cherry paid for entry tickets.

Most castles contained items related to the castle era, or they lay in ruins. This one had bare rooms.

"Why are the rooms empty?" Joanna asked.

Cherry read a notice on the wall. "The castle's owners renovated and carried out repairs. The wood needs to dry before they can move in furniture." Instead of antiques, contemporary art pieces hung on the walls. The three of them wandered through the original rooms, studying the pictures. Joanna ran everywhere, shouting when she decided Cherry and Martinos were moving too slow.

"Hey, little one," Martinos said, grabbing for Joanna's hand as she tore past them. "There's no need to run everywhere. You're tiring us out."

Joanna tugged at her cap, allowing Cherry to see her grin. "Okay."

"What should I take photos of today?" Cherry pulled out her phone and waited for Joanna to decide.

"The castle from the outside."

Obediently, Cherry snapped the required photos.

"Can you show me how to work the photo machine?" Martinos asked.

"Sure. You can be our photographer today." She showed Martinos how to snap a photo and to do a selfie. "Don't you have something similar on your island?"

"No, our people continue to live in the ways of their ancestors. You have many machines to make things while we own weapons to defend ourselves and utensils to eat our food. Farmers and blacksmiths, bakers, and other merchants possess their tools of the trade."

"Your world reminds me of a medieval society. Remind me to show you some of our history sites online once we return to the cottage. Have things changed from the time when you retreated to the islands?"

"Our people are big on traditions. In my opinion, the lack of change helps the dragons to maintain their rule."

"Interesting," Cherry said. "From the dragons' point of view, why mess with a system that works for them."

With the castle explored and the photos snapped, they strolled to the cafe for an ice cream cone.

Martinos stared at the cone she handed him. "What do I do with this?"

"Eat it," Joanna shouted.

Cherry smiled at him, her heart beating a fraction faster as a naughty idea occurred to her. "Lick it. Like this." She ran her tongue over the scoop of chocolate ice cream. She kept her gaze on Martinos while she repeated the move.

His eyes narrowed, and he continued to stare at her, his mouth firm.

She took another long lick, and this time Martinos growled.

"Your ice cream is melting," Joanna told him.

The chocolate ice cream dripped down his hand and forearm.

"Lick your cone, Martinos," Cherry said and winked at him.

"Minx," he whispered.

A giggle escaped Cherry—to her surprise. "Eat the ice cream, Martinos. It's delicious."

With his gaze on her, he licked the frozen confection, and a sound of approval rumbled in his throat. "It is tasty." He partook with more enthusiasm, and without warning, the scoop rolled off his cone and fell, splat, on the ground. He muttered something under his breath and turned to her, distress in his expression. "It dropped."

She gave a solemn nod. "It does that. Be careful."

"What should I do?"

"We'll get you another one. Would you like to try a different flavor?"

"Please."

Cherry handed over a ten-pound note. "Ask for a single scoop of whatever flavor you want to try."

Martinos was back in five minutes. This time, he'd chosen lime with chocolate chips.

"I liked the color," he said.

She sent him an impish grin, reveling in the sensual teasing. Martinos had bolstered her confidence, and she hadn't experienced such happiness in a long time. "Lick with caution."

"I will," Martinos said, and this time, he proceeded with care.

By the time he'd finished his cone, lime ice cream covered his mouth and chin.

Cherry glanced from Martinos to Joanna, her amusement growing. "Boys are messy when they eat ice cream. You both have it smeared on your faces."

She reached into her handbag for the travel pack of wipes. "Jo, let me clean your face."

Joanna kicked the dirt with her red sneaker. "Boys have dirty faces."

"I don't want to look at your ice cream face." She leaned closer.

"Do you want me to spread rumors you have bubble baths?"

"Aunt Cherry!" Joanna stared at her with wounded eyes. "That's mean!"

Cherry hid her amusement and glanced around. She noticed a mother with a wipe in hand, attacking the ice cream on her son's chin. "That lady is cleaning her son's face."

"All right," Joanna agreed, although she was pouting. She was taking this disguise business seriously.

"You can clean my face," Martinos said, and his eyes gleamed with mischief.

"Can't you do it yourself?"

"I can't see the dirty bits."

"Knock off that innocent tone, Martinos," she said, but laughter bubbled up inside her. That lightness and happiness again. The excitement of what might happen between them tonight. With Rena putting off her arrival for longer, they had the luxury of privacy once Joanna retired for the evening.

His brows rose in a silent challenge, and once she'd finished with Joanna, she approached Martinos. "I can't believe the weight you've put on even in a few days." She dabbed at the green ice cream, her attention drawn by his lips. They were firm, the bottom one fuller than the top. Her stomach hollowed out as she recalled the magic they'd wrought on her body.

"If you stare much harder, I will kiss you," he murmured, simmering promise inherent in his words.

She swallowed hard. "I want you to kiss me."

He cursed under his breath and stepped nearer to cup her face. "You're a witch, casting a spell on me. A siren who rescued me from the sea."

"No, I'm an ordinary woman," she whispered, instinctively raising her head to offer her mouth.

Martinos groaned and laid a butterfly kiss on her mouth, stepping back way too fast for Cherry's taste. Her fingers traveled to her lips, and his brown gaze darkened as he took the damp wipe from her.

"Later," he mouthed.

"Where are we going next?" Joanna piped up.

"Let's go for a drive around the island. Once we get out of town, Martinos can have a turn driving."

"Really?" he asked.

"Yes. I'm certain we'll find a way for you to go home, but just in case, learn how to do as much as you can on your own." Curiosity made her add, "What if you can't return to the Dragon Isles? Will that upset you?"

"I haven't considered it," he confessed. "What I want most is to free my dragon. There's a hollow part inside me, one that never fades."

He'd leave her.

Cherry fought to maintain her inquisitive countenance. It was time to cease her daydreams of happy-ever-after. She understood their differences. Why couldn't she let that go? She was sure her mother would lecture her on that should Cherry ever share these details with her. Which reminded her, she should check in with her mother and make sure everything was okay with her bookstore. She'd do it later tonight. Give herself time to work out exactly what to tell her parent.

"Let's go," Cherry said.

When they arrived back at the car park, they piled into the car and drove through town.

"There is the man we saw yesterday," Joanna said, waving out the window.

"Where?" Martinos demanded.

"I see him," Cherry said. "Over to the right. He's staring right at us."

"The bastard is smirking."

"He recognized you," Cherry said with certainty.

"I think so. Stay away from him. Nemyr is dangerous."

"He's walking through town and away from us. What do you want to do? Should we return home?" Cherry asked.

"I don't believe he'd hurt either you or Joanna and draw attention to himself. We should carry on with our drive. It doesn't appear as if he's shifting to his dragon form while he's on Holy Island."

Cherry understood what Martinos didn't say. The dragon-man would hurt or even kill Martinos if he had the chance.

"Is he a terrible man?" Joanna asked.

"Yes," Martinos said. "If you see him, run away and hide."

"Why?" Joanna asked.

Cherry exchanged a look with Martinos. The last thing she wanted was to frighten Joanna.

"He broke the law," Martinos said. "But he's astute and avoided getting caught."

"Why didn't you tell on him?" Joanna asked.

What should they tell her? She was a child and one who should retain her innocence.

"He is an important person," Martinos said. "People didn't believe he'd broken the law."

Cherry watched Joanna in the rear-vision mirror. Liza's daughter furrowed her brow. "Is he bad like my daddy?"

Cherry's heart squeezed in compassion for the child. A kid of her age shouldn't have concerns regarding grown-up stuff. Heck, Cherry was withholding information about Liza. A reminder to call the police for another update. "Yes," she said. "But it's not for you to worry. Martinos and I will keep you safe. Okay?"

"Yes, Aunt Cherry."

"Excellent," Cherry said, and she continued driving, following a sign that led to the beaches on the north of the island. "We'll do a loop back to here and park. I thought we'd do the nature walk."

"What about the naughty man?" Joanna piped up.

"He's probably going home," Martinos said. "Let's enjoy our

day."

"I haven't been here before," Cherry said. "The dunes and mudflats are home to lots of seabirds. Joanna, why don't you see how many types you can count?"

This new game kept Joanna occupied and allowed Cherry to voice her questions in an undertone. "Does he know where we're living? Does he travel to and from your world to here whenever he feels like it? Why is he here? What does he want?"

"I don't know the answers to any of those questions," Martinos whispered. "I'd follow him if I could, but I don't want to leave you open to danger."

"But what if he can help you to get home?" Cherry's heart ached on uttering the words. "You have to try every avenue."

"I know," Martinos replied. "But I need to free my dragon to have any chance of survival." Frustration shone in his eyes. "I can't protect you from another dragon with my beast contained. Not when Nemyr can shift at will."

"Why hasn't he?"

"I don't know, but my best guess is he needs something here and wishes secrecy while undertaking his mission."

"So many unanswered questions."

"Yes," Martinos said.

"Would it be better to return to the cottage?"

"As far as I can see, Nemyr hasn't followed us. Let's continue with our day."

"Would he have traveled to the mainland? Could he drive?"

"When we spotted him yesterday, the causeway was closed," Martinos said, his expression thoughtful. "Maybe you're right, and he was returning from the mainland."

"He wasn't carrying packages."

"No, but he wore a pack on his back last time we saw him. He wore one today too."

"Did you notice foreign goods on your island? Wait, stupid question. You were in the castle dungeon."

"Cherry, I don't know. Nemyr could do any number of things over here. The possibilities are endless. For all we know, he and his coconspirators wish to conquer those on the mainland."

"You think they've decided it's time for dragons to inhabit the mainland again?"

Martinos scowled. "Anything is possible."

"Do you want to try driving now?"

"It's best if you drive while Nemyr is on the island," Martinos said.

"What happens if he brings reinforcements?"

"If that's the case, you'll need to leave. Take Joanna to a safe place elsewhere on the mainland, as far from here as possible."

Almost two hours later, Cherry drove toward their cottage. Both she and Martinos scanned the streets, searching for Nemyr.

"The tide is in now," Cherry said.

"Yes, but on which side of the water is Nemyr standing?"

"Look, trees," Joanna said, breaking the tension in the vehicle.

Cherry slowed and pulled over, so they could see where Joanna was pointing.

"Yew trees," Martinos whispered, awe in his tone.

"Is there something special about yew trees?"

"They're magical with extraordinary powers. The druids revere the trees and use them in their spells."

Cherry frowned. "I recall watching a documentary. Yews are dangerous. Their leaves and seeds and the sawdust from the yew wood are poisonous to humans and pets."

"Even so, the trees hold age and wisdom within their trunks. I should've thought of them when Rena mentioned magic trees. Our ancestors planted yews in groves near churches and graveyards. The ones we can see look like a grove. Many trees within a confined area provide significant power for the druids."

"What do we do next?" Cherry asked.

"We should go home where you and Joanna can stay safe. Nemyr may be using the yew trees as a portal."

Cherry winged a glare his way. "You shouldn't be alone. What if something happens and I can't help you?"

"Someone is standing by the trees," Martinos said without warning.

Cherry swung her gaze back in that direction.

"A woman," Martinos said.

Cherry straightened and opened her door. "Rena! What is she

doing here? I thought she was staying in Edinburgh for longer."

"Cherry, wait," Martinos called. But Cherry didn't listen. She strode at first, then she started running. Tension pushed at his chest. Fear.

An emotion he hadn't felt for years and not for another being.

Cherry had wriggled into his heart in such a short time, and she mattered to him. He glanced at Joanna, not wanting to leave her alone.

Cherry ran right at the other woman. They wrapped their arms around one another and embraced. A fraction of the apprehension in Martinos faded as feminine laughter and chatter floated to him.

"That's Aunt Rena," Joanna said. "Can I say hello to her?"

Martinos scanned the grove, searching for danger signs. "Yes, you can go." He turned, but Joanna had exited the car and was on her way to meet Cherry and her friend, Rena.

Martinos leaped out of the vehicle, uncomfortable with Joanna and Cherry too far away from him. The back of his neck prickled, yet he couldn't see a reason for this internal alarm.

Joanna reached the two women and hugged Cherry's friend. Martinos hustled, increasing his pace to a jog.

"Is everything all right?" he asked.

"I dreamed I needed to come today, so I did," Rena said. "I'm so pleased to see you, Joanna."

"My name is Jo," Joanna said in a loud voice.

Martinos caught Cherry's gaze and her twitch of lips. He

grinned at her in return.

"Long story," Cherry murmured to Rena. "I'll explain later. What are you doing here? You didn't mention a dream when we spoke earlier."

"I fell asleep again," Rena said. "My sleep hasn't been restful. I booked my ticket and came once I was positive I'd dodged Tony. I traveled on a local bus."

"You should've called. We would've picked you up from the town," Cherry said.

Rena shrugged. "David told me to search for magic trees. Yew trees are as magic as it gets." She gestured at the yews, her eyes widening and a gasp escaping her.

Martinos spun around to stare at the yew trees, every muscle poised to fight off Nemyr despite his physical disadvantages. The arrival wasn't Nemyr, but there was a man standing on the edge of the grove. Martinos glanced back at Rena and Cherry.

Rena's hand flew to her chest, and she squeezed her eyes shut for an instant. When she opened them again, her expression was dazed. "David," she whispered.

CHAPTER 12

The Dragon Seizes Control

Martinos narrowed his eyes, squinting at the new arrival. His breath quickened, the constant knot in his belly drawing even tighter.

A druid.

At last.

He found his legs moving without volition, and seconds later, he had his hands on the druid, shaking him. "Free me now."

"Martinos," Cherry yelled.

"Leave him alone," Rena cried. "He didn't place the spell on you."

Joanna pushed between Rena and Cherry. "What are you doing? Do boys fight all the time?"

It was Joanna's appalled comment that pierced the red haze shrouding Martinos's mind. He slackened his grip and forced his legs to move back half a step. "I'm sorry," he croaked, shame sending heat to the tips of his ears.

The druid rubbed his throat, his gaze watchful as he retreated a fraction. Intelligence blazed in his eyes.

"David, are you okay?" At David's nod, Rena wheeled on Martinos. "Why did you do that? He's come to help."

"Something is putrid in the state of druids," Martinos snapped. "Nan and my so-called friends set me up, and the druids willingly trapped my dragon. I lost part of myself when that happened. On my escape, I ended up here on the mainland, a place I shouldn't be. And now, we've spotted Nemyr, The Scary, apparently coming and going at will."

"But that doesn't give you an excuse to attack him." Rena glowered, fierce in her defense of the druid.

"No." David placed his hand on Rena's arm and smiled in reassurance. "He has a right to his anger. Martinos is correct in thinking something is out of sync in our world. I investigated as much as I could before traveling here." He sent a pleading glance to Martinos. "I mean you no harm and want to help free your dragon. I have researched the spells, and I have one that should work."

Eagerness rose in Martinos. "When can you do the chant?"

Martinos forced himself to ignore the way the color fled from Cherry's face. She didn't understand, couldn't understand how much the loss of his dragon had affected him. How he only felt half alive, even though he'd attempted not to dwell on the harsh punishment meted out to him.

He'd succeeded.

Until now.

Now that he had a slight hope of returning to normal, his suppressed anger had exploded inside him. He curled his hands into fists at his sides, digging his fingernails into his palms to focus on the present. "What do I do?" *There, he'd managed polite.*

"We'll walk to the middle of the yew grove. That's where I need to chant the spell I've written to remove the armband and free your dragon."

"Martinos." Joanna tugged on his T-shirt. "You didn't tell me you were a dragon."

Rena clapped her hand over Joanna's mouth, snaring the child's attention. "It's a big secret, Joanna. No one can know, or it will place Martinos in danger. Do you want the police to take him away?"

Cherry croaked a protest.

"It's fine," Martinos said and crouched in front of Joanna. "I am a dragon, but I don't come from your world. Your Aunt Rena is right. We can't tell other people because they believe dragons are dangerous."

"You are when you're grumpy," Joanna said.

Unsure of what to say, he ran with the truth. "I'm sorry I've shouted today and fought against David. I'm worried my dragon has died."

Joanna hugged him hard, her features holding sympathy. "I'm sorry your dragon is sick."

"The druid will help me."

"Is he a secret too?"

"Yes." Martinos hugged the child back, her sweet innocence bringing shame washing through him again. "You listen to your Aunt Cherry and Aunt Rena, and do what they tell you."

"I will." Joanna stepped back.

Martinos sucked in a breath and nodded at the druid. "Has the yew grove turned into a portal?"

"That is my suspicion," David said. "We must hurry. I'm uncertain of the numbers of dragons traveling in this manner. We could both die if we're not careful."

With a curt nod, Martinos followed David deeper into the circle of yews. Mindful of the tree's toxicity, Martinos refrained from touching the foliage or bark.

Up ahead, the druid stopped and spun in a slow circle. A scowl dug into his youthful features. "This open spot should do for our purposes."

"Will your spell work?"

The druid's dark brows drew together until they resembled a flat line. "I am hesitant to forecast the outcome."

Martinos gave a curt nod. These days, he valued honesty. "I appreciate you risking your position to help me."

"It's the right thing to do." The druid opened a pouch he wore at his waist, and he pulled out a bottle filled with various herbs. When the druid handed it to him, Martinos recognized the bright red of yew berries inside and the sprig of rosemary. The identity of the other herbs, sticks, and plants remained a mystery.

"What is this for?"

"It's a protective talisman. I was in a hurry and didn't have time to weave it into a brooch for you to wear. Place the jar within your pocket. I will chant the spell. I warn you, your armband will heat, and I suspect it might burn. Whatever you do, you can't move. You must stand as still as possible and focus on your dragon. Call him. Summon him. Plea for him to return. You must picture him in your mind and implore him to awaken from his long sleep."

"What if he's dead? I never feel him move. I haven't for years."

David frowned again, his intense concentration making him appear older than Martinos's first guess. The color of his robe—black—showed his junior rank within the order of druids.

"Even if your spell doesn't work, I thank you for risking your safety to help me. From what I understand, your order is strict. If your elders catch you, they will make you suffer."

"I loathe injustice," the druid spat. "I joined the order because I wished to help those weaker, not make them suffer. Lately, the senior druids—some of them—are abusing their power."

"As are the dragons."

"That is a worry." The druid shifted his stance and squared his shoulders. "Are you ready to begin? Remember, you must *not* move. I must concentrate the spell on the armband, and I do not wish you to suffer more than necessary."

Martinos squared his shoulders and pictured his dragon. "Ready."

The druid started his chant, his words fluid and rapid and spoken in an old Celtic language. Martinos mindspoke with his dragon as if he were present, praising his strength and his courage. Imploring him to come out to play. They'd take a prolonged flight and relish the air currents puffing against their protective scales, their wings. *"Come out. I wish to see you and ensure you're healthy."*

The band heated, the warm metal becoming hotter and hotter. His skin sizzled with discomfort, disrupting his flow of calm concentration. Mindful of the druid's words, Martinos forced his focus back to his dragon. He pictured each red scale on his chest and tail. He recalled the triumphant bugle he'd issue during their next hunt. He zoned out, his faith in his dragon pushing aside the torment attacking his upper arm.

Sweat broke out on his forehead. It dripped into his eyes, blinding him. Every instinct had him wanting to swipe away the sting. He refrained. Instead, he continued to picture his dragon. He talked to him and told him how much he'd missed him during his time in the dungeon. *"Please return and make us whole again."*

Martinos told his dragon of Cherry: he described her beauty, her red hair, her delectable soft skin, and her cinnamon freckles. He mindspoke about his liking of her. He needed his dragon to visit and meet Cherry. He required his dragon's blessing to ensure he'd chosen the right woman for them.

Martinos paused in his thoughts. How did he entice his dragon from his solitary prison? The instant Martinos paused, the fiery heat emanating from the armband almost took him out at the knees. Agony blazed through him, an excruciating bolt of pain that shredded his concentration.

Martinos groaned and shook away his fogginess, determined to give this druid every chance of completing his spell. He had to do his part or risk harming the druid and perhaps the women and child.

His dragon.

He was a red dragon, forceful and arrogant.

A part of Martinos wondered at his dragon's attitude to the new Martinos.

Too bad.

Martinos refused to fight for his dragon's approval. They were a team, and no matter where they were or who they dealt with, they worked together. Somehow, they'd bind again and use their strength for good, for improvements.

Revenge might have been top of his mind, but his time with

Cherry had shown him retaliation wouldn't return the wasted years nor help the young woman who'd suffered so that others could frame him for the crime. Payback wasn't possible anyhow, not when his dragon refused to answer his summons to return and unite.

Martinos paused and repeated his one-sided conversation. Once he finished, he mentally stumbled, at a loss. His dragon remained stubbornly silent.

Once again, he became aware of the temperature of his band. It blistered his arm, the metal glowing a golden red. The stench of burning filled his nostrils. Martinos trembled, his knees weakening, protesting his upright position.

The druid's lyrical words faltered, and Martinos, somehow, remained standing.

"Please, please return to me. If you don't, we will both continue to suffer. I need your strength, your courage, your arrogance to get me through this task. You must use your muscles to help me break the weakened metal of the armband. We must work together before we both burn alive. Please, my mighty dragon. Grant me this boon."

The druid continued with his spell, his voice growing hoarse from overuse.

"My dragon, come. The three of us must work together. The druid. The fallen man. The mighty dragon."

Martinos experienced a flutter in his belly. His focus fractured, and the pain was worse than anything he'd ever experienced.

Wisps of smoke rose from the armband. He smelled cooking flesh and the metallic burning of the band. The acrid taste of magic singed the back of his throat. Martinos sensed this was his last chance.

"Do you want us to both die?" he demanded. *"You must fight. We must battle to gain freedom. I don't want to die. I want to mate with Cherry. Somehow, we'll make it work even though she comes from the mainland. You'll love her."*

Yes! The flutter in his belly repeated, growing robust and familiar. *"Yes, my dragon,"* Martinos crooned. *"Yes!"*

Power exploded inside him, his body flexing, his muscles bulging against the agonizing pain and his burning flesh.

The druid's voice grew louder, his words more distinctive. Potent power poured from him.

"Yes, my dragon. It is time to break this curse. It is time for freedom."

The armband gave a distinct crack. As that sound registered, his dragon flared inside him, forcing his way from his human form with a roar of furious anger. *Up, up, up.* Scales exploded on his body, a rush of power snapping the armband, ripping his clothes.

He was free.

His dragon exploded with fury, stealing Martinos's breath and halting his anguished pleas.

Now pain of an uncommon sort filled him.

Disorientation. A breathlessness. A lack of control.

His dragon shoved aside his human half, rising into the air, the tatters of his shredding clothing dropping in a trail behind him.

"Where are you going?" Martinos cried through the channel they used to communicate.

His dragon didn't reply. Instead, he soared higher, his large nostrils flaring, his fury at being contained for so long fueling his behavior.

His dragon's rage was an uncomfortable buzz in his brain. His arm ached and throbbed, his shift to dragon form not alleviating a scrap of the pain lashing him.

Where was the druid?

Martinos hadn't seen what had happened to him, and he prayed his transformation hadn't injured the man. He—*they*—owed the druid much.

The dragon cocked his head and dove lower, eagerness and purpose in his flight now.

Martinos stared out of his dragon's eyes, seeing what his dragon saw.

His heart twisted, and fear burst into life.

"No. No, you can't hurt the women. The child. They are innocents. Blameless. Please, don't hurt them. I implore you."

His dragon maintained his dive, extended his talons while Martinos fought to exert control. Authority. His dragon never faltered. He let out a triumphant roar. It attracted attention. *Of course it did.* Cherry and Rena weren't used to dragons arrowing through the sky. They didn't understand the dangers, hadn't learned to hide or flee when dragons flew overhead.

Cherry.

His heart ached for her, but he could do nothing to save her from his dragon.

His dragon plucked Cherry off the ground, grasping her in his talons. She shrieked as they rose into the sky.

Martinos spotted Rena, relief filling him when he glimpsed her comforting Joanna.

His dragon flew away from Holy Island, out over the North Sea. While the druid had been chanting, the clouds had closed in, the blackness of them signaling an upcoming storm.

Cherry.

By Lodar, if his dragon had injured the woman he loved, he had no way to atone for this disaster.

He couldn't see Cherry, couldn't hear her above the wind rushing past his ears. Martinos focused on talking to his dragon, but the creature was in control. Part of Martinos understood. He'd experienced a similar joy at escaping the dungeon.

"Different," roared his dragon, his fury whipping at Martinos's mind.

Rage consumed his dragon, and the bitter iron taste of it filled his throat and emerged in a belly-busting flare of heat. His flames burst through the darkening sky, and Martinos prayed no humans witnessed his dragon's tantrum.

He worried about Cherry, every part of him praying she was uninjured and that the fresh icy air didn't chill her beyond help.

The air thickened, and his dragon faltered, his wings straining to push through the obstruction. It was like flying through thick honey, but his dragon burst through as fast as they'd encountered the strange phenomenon. Martinos thought he'd heard a scream.

His dragon ignored him and refused to share a mind, refused to let Martinos control any part of his body, refused to protect Cherry.

The farther they traveled, the more Martinos worried over Cherry's state of health. Although she was a courageous woman, this unexpected flight must fill her with terror.

By Lodar, he had no idea of their location or where his out-of-control dragon intended to take them.

He stared ahead, his vision restricted to the direction in which his dragon pointed. He struggled for a clue—any clue as to where his dragon might have flown. His eyes strained to pierce the gloom. Drops of rain drove against his hide. His dragon blinked, cutting off Martinos's one avenue of knowledge.

His body ached while his arm throbbed unmercifully. His beast form had fractured his concentration. He'd lost his power and any hope of saving Cherry. Now that his dragon was free, he was intent on punishing Martinos for keeping him contained. His dragon didn't care that none of the blame belonged to Martinos.

And because of this, he'd seized Cherry.

Martinos would never forgive his dragon for this act of revenge. *Never.*

"Oh, my god," Rena muttered, panic in her voice.

Cherry's eyes widened, shock rooting her feet to the ground. A huge red dragon barreled toward them, its talons extending as the creature neared.

"Run," Rena screamed, shoving at Joanna and nudging her niece to action.

Cherry raced behind them, running faster than she'd ever sprinted in her life. Rena and Joanna ducked into the yew grove, but the path Cherry took had her emerging from the trees and racing into the open.

An instant later, the dragon plucked her off the ground, her terrified scream echoing around her and falling away in the rush of air. The dragon lifted up, up, up into the sky and set a course away from Holy Island. Fear beat in Cherry's ears, the dragon's talons a cage around her body. What if the dragon dropped her?

Lordy, a part of her had doubted Martinos's word of a dragon living inside him, incarcerated by the druid's magical spell. She hadn't truly understood what that might mean. Now she was learning the hard way. Heck, it was a long way down. She doubted she'd survive the drop to the sea.

Her pulse raced a little faster. Where was the dragon taking her? What did he want?

She was certain Rena and Joanna were safe. Rena would care for Liza's daughter with her last breath, and of that, Cherry was confident.

Her thoughts were a mass of writhing panic, and she had no idea—not a clue—of what she might do to save herself. And Martinos. Where did he go when the dragon took over his body? Did he have any authority? She released a weak gasp and wished she'd asked more questions while she'd had a chance. A shiver racked her body, the chill of an approaching storm zapping any remaining warmth from the day. She'd worn light clothes because they'd been walking and the morning had been sunny.

A mistake, as it had turned out.

The dragon angled its flight path. It slowed for an instant before picking up speed again.

Panic shot through her. The barrier? The one between their worlds?

She had a bookshop to run. Responsibilities. She and Rena were accountable for Joanna's safety. The girl counted on them to protect her from Tony. She still hadn't rung the police to learn the status of the search for Liza. Tears stung her eyes, the constant blast of air partially responsible but also the emotions boiling over inside her.

She couldn't go missing like Liza—reported as dead because no one had found her body. Martinos's world sounded so bloodthirsty and archaic. Not the place for an innocent human.

The dragon continued his frenzied race through the sky. Rain pelted her, sticking her clothes to her wet skin. She strained to see through the growing darkness. More sea with waves and whitecaps. She turned her head a fraction. Land. Was that land?

The dragon flew in that direction. *Yes!* They were heading for an island. Judging by the smoke billowing from one mountain, it was Smoking Isle. Martinos's home. *Popsicles!* She bit her lip and prayed to every god she knew that they didn't come in contact with Martinos's nasty sister. She spotted a building surrounded by lots of other smaller ones. The largest appeared fortified—resembling an old Norman castle with square towers.

The dragon soared downward. Its substantial red wings acted as a brake, reducing the speed of its flight.

It touched down on one talon and opened the other, freeing her from its tight grip.

Cherry toppled forward, falling heavily on her hands and knees. She groaned as her kneecaps collided with gravel. One oversized dragon foot nudged her out of the way, and she rolled without volition.

The dragon lifted its head and roared. Flames shot from the creature's great maw, and if anyone had asked, Cherry would've told them it was a victory cry. A dragon reclaiming its home.

She dragged herself to a sitting position, and when the dragon did nothing to stop her, pushed to her feet. She made out the features of men and women staring from windows. Fear shadowed their faces.

Cherry swallowed.

"We're not here to hurt you," she shouted.

The dragon turned its colossal head to stare at her. It sniffed, raising its snout with more than a hint of arrogance.

"We will not hurt them," she stated. "My guess is your sister has terrorized them enough. You need to repair bridges, not smash them to smithereens."

The dragon stared at her, its golden eyes flickering. Disdain dripped off the beast along with haughtiness.

"They had nothing to do with your…" At the last moment, she decided on diplomacy, but she struggled with a word to describe the crime against him. "Absence." She offered a weak smile as the dragon sneered at her and opened its great maw to expose wicked sharp teeth.

All the better to bite her.

Fear flashed through her, and she retreated.

The dragon snorted, and she realized he was playing, trying to panic her.

Irritation flooded her then, and she bounded forward to poke the dragon on its broad chest. "I didn't ask to come here. You brought me against my will." She poked him again for good measure. "You can huff and puff all you want, but you don't scare me. Martinos was worried about what had happened to his people. You must be too."

The dragon sent a fiery flare of flames into the sky and stomped his front legs. Finally, he grabbed her in his right talon and seized her, startling free another squeak of terror.

Teasing the dragon and offering up backchat. *Bad, bad idea!*

CHAPTER 13

A Power Struggle

Another cry escaped Cherry, and she bit her bottom lip to stop a third. She refused to show her anxiety to this oafish dragon. "What are you doing?" she shouted.

The dragon shunted her through a doorway and retreated. The creature took to the air and disappeared, leaving her stunned and alone in a strange place.

"Sir. Sir!" an elderly man called. "I saw you arrive with the dragon. Are you well?"

Cherry turned around, relieved to find the locals were friendly.

The man froze a few feet from her. "You're a woman."

Give the man a prize. "Is that a problem?"

"No. No, of course not." He stared at her, his bushy gray brows drawing together. "You are not from here. Your clothes." He gestured at her jeans.

"No." Cherry decided not to offer details. News that dragons and humans were crossing the border between their worlds might not go well for her.

"Where are you from? One of the other islands?"

"Yes, the dragon grabbed me and flew me here."

"Who was the dragon? He was too far away for me to recognize."

Again, Cherry hesitated. Martinos might not be popular here, the locals judging him without understanding the details. "I do not know."

"This is most irregular," the man muttered. "First, Nandag leaves to meet her betrothed, and the next thing we hear, the wedding is canceled. Leonidas married someone else. Now Nandag has disappeared, and no one has heard from her. We expected her to return. We are at a loss."

Interesting. She wanted to ask questions but bit her tongue to contain her curiosity. Best to wait and collect details as they emerged. She strode to the door and peered outside.

The dragon was no longer in sight, and with darkness falling, it appeared she'd be spending the night.

"Who is in charge while Nandag is away?" Cherry asked. "I should speak to them."

"Nandag's closest confidants traveled with her to Hissing Isle.

Only humans stayed."

Cherry nodded. Perfect. If she couldn't return to Holy Island, she'd blend with the existing workforce. "Have you experienced problems?"

"Oh, no. We continue with our routines. We are running short of funds to procure food. I'm afraid we celebrated the betrothal of our mistress and had a sizeable party." He glanced over his shoulder and leaned closer. "Our mistress would disapprove."

How did they expect to hide the party from Nandag? She glanced around the room and noticed the layer of dust covering the floor. "Are you sure you're doing everything as usual?"

"Most of the servants left when they did not receive their wages."

Cherry's warning antenna rose. "How many remain?"

"Three," the elderly man replied.

"But I saw more than three people peering out at me during my arrival."

"They came to visit and returned to the village once the dragon departed."

"What is your name?"

"I am Alfred, the head butler."

Holy Batman! She pressed her lips together and suppressed the Batman joke that came to mind. This elderly gentleman was nothing like the butlers of her imagination, the ones she'd read about in her favorite books or seen in the movies. "I am Cherry. Pleased to meet you, Alfred. It is too late for me to travel. Is there somewhere I could sleep for tonight?"

Alfred frowned. "It is not my place to invite strangers into Nandag's home."

"I understand," Cherry said. "However, these are not normal times. You alluded to the strangeness of recent happenings. There must be one room I could claim for the evening."

The butler pursed his lips. "Very well. You may use one of the staff chambers for this evening."

"If you could add a meal, I'd be willing to help with tasks to earn my keep."

The butler nodded immediately, which raised her suspicions. She refrained from blurting the questions that lined up in her mind like soldiers. The butler had economized with the truth. She'd wait until Martinos shifted. He could clear up the problems and assemble a staff to clean his home.

"Is there something for me to eat now? A cup of tea?"

"Of course," Alfred said, maintaining his dignity throughout his lies. "This way. We'd all welcome tea."

Cherry followed Alfred deeper into the building and noted the dust covering every surface. He turned along a narrow corridor. In the dim-lit space, she stumbled over a broken tile and almost face-planted. "Popsicles!" She caught herself on her hands and knees. *Again.* A sharp dart of pain radiated from her grazed palms and skinned knees, and Cherry bit her lip to contain her whimper.

"Watch for the broken tiles," Alfred said.

"Thank you," Cherry said sweetly through gritted teeth. She'd broken a kneecap for sure. She picked herself up and limped after Alfred.

He led her into a kitchen where a woman of his age sat at a scarred wooden table. The woman wore her gray hair arranged in a coil atop her head, and a few wisps had escaped during her day. Interest lit her pale blue eyes when Alfred and Cherry entered the kitchen. A fire burned in the hearth, and a black kettle sat to the side. Cherry didn't spot a single modern convenience. Surely there was at least one? Martinos had told her this, but seeing the evidence brought home the truth. This kitchen came straight from the pages of an English history book.

"This is Cherry. The red dragon dropped her at the door."

"Where did everyone go?" Cherry asked, interested to learn if the answer changed.

"The dragon's arrival scared them," the woman said. "They returned to the village in the hope the dragon left them alone."

"Your name is?"

"Betty," the woman said. "I'm Alfred's wife. We have been looking after the mansion as best we can since Nandag disappeared."

Cherry shot a glance at Alfred. He wore a scowl.

"Don't tell her everything," he warned.

"Why?" Betty asked. "Nandag left us on our own to do our best with no funds."

"Why did you stay?" Cherry asked.

"We have nowhere else to go," Betty said. "Now that we're older, it's difficult to start over with nothing. We've worked here since our twenties."

Cherry nodded. She presumed this property was Martinos's family home. She couldn't do anything or go anywhere until either the dragon returned or Martinos arrived. So she'd stay here and help Alfred and Betty give the place a spring clean. If Martinos didn't turn up, she'd walk to the nearest village and assemble further information.

Martinos required details concerning the activities during his absence. He'd want facts to make decisions, so she'd help him.

When he finally deigned to speak with her, she'd shriek at him for kidnapping her first. That was a given. Unfortunately, or perhaps, fortunately, she'd come to like the great lug. No, honesty—at least to herself. She loved him, and after she gave him grief, she'd help him set things in order here at his family home.

"Alfred promised me a cup of tea," Cherry said.

Betty frowned. "We are short of supplies. I don't think—"

"Give the lass tea," Alfred interrupted. "The dragon dumped her here and left. She's in shock after the way he gripped her in his talons. Hot, sweet tea will settle her nerves."

"Humph," Betty said. "I know your plan, husband. It's you who desires tea to settle their nerves. I'm surprised young Cherry isn't weeping uncontrollably after the beast carted her here, but she seems calm while you, old man, look fit to drop."

"Never," Alfred said, his shoulders straightening in affront.

The pair bickered amicably while Cherry took matters into her own hands. She spotted a kettle. "Where do I find the water?"

"In the well outside," Alfred said. "I will bring water shortly." He turned away and left the kitchen via a different door.

"You don't have running water?" Cherry asked, shocked.

"No. Our mistress didn't see the need to have running water in the kitchen when the well is right outside the door."

"What about water for washing? Clothes and for bathing."

"Mistress Nan has a bathroom with piped water. It's marvelous since boiling water comes from the taps too. We heat the water in large coppers for the laundry."

"That is archaic," Cherry muttered. "I'll have words with Martinos."

"Martinos?"

It appeared there was nothing wrong with Betty's hearing. "Yes, my ah..." She frowned, wondering how she should describe Martinos and how much information she should give Betty. Not much, she decided. It was up to Martinos to tell his people whatever he wished them to know, although they had probably heard of his imprisonment. "My friend," she said. "How long ago did Nandag leave?"

"Over a month now. She has never been gone for so long and never without leaving someone in charge."

A suspicion formed in Cherry. What if Nandag had abandoned this house? "Did everyone leave together?"

"No," Betty said.

"The majority left three weeks before Mistress Nandag. They informed us they were arranging matters relating to the betrothal. Mistress Nandag left with her party of close friends and her servants four weeks later. They flew in dragon form to travel to Hissing Isle. The lower dragons arranged the passage of belongings via ship. They left on the same day."

"I see," Cherry said, glad that Betty was more forthcoming than her husband. "How many employees did Mistress Nandag leave here with you when she left?"

"Six," Betty replied. "Alfred and I plus four other female servants. My best friend, Gertrude, calls, and Alfred's friends drop by to visit. They were here when you arrived with the dragon."

"I see," Cherry repeated. "Did Nandag and the others take their belongings with them?"

Betty frowned. "I don't know. Two of the girls cleaned the mansion bedrooms and public areas. The other two girls helped me with meals and laundry."

Alfred arrived back carrying a dripping bucket of water. Betty clucked and hustled over to her husband to relieve him of the pail.

"Look now, Alfred," she scolded. "Don't you be spilling water on my clean floor."

Cherry claimed a chair and waited while Betty bossed Alfred.

The kitchen was spotless compared to the rest of the house.

"Don't just stand there. Get out the mugs for tea. The jug of milk and a bowl of sugar lumps. Hurry now. We have a guest waiting."

Alfred grumbled under his breath but did as asked.

Cherry used the respite to ponder all she'd learned.

The water boiled rapidly over the fire, and soon Betty placed a pot of tea on the table.

"Gertrude brought a dish of jam tarts," Betty said. "We'll have one each with our tea."

"Do we have to share?" Alfred mumbled. "I wanted one for supper."

Betty tsked and ignored her grumpy husband. She shunted a shiny strawberry tart in Cherry's direction. "Start on that while the tea steeps. The quality tea from Perfume Isle deserves proper brewing. I can't abide by wishy-washy tea."

"No," Cherry agreed, still deep in thought. She had a theory. As soon as she'd finished her tea, she'd test it out, but she'd bet her rare book of Wordsworth poems that something was very wrong in this mansion.

Once Betty poured her a mug of tea, Cherry added a dash of milk and one sugar lump. She stirred it and clinked her teaspoon against the side. They drank and ate in silence.

"Did your Mistress Nandag leave you money to buy food and to pay your wages?"

"She mentioned it," Betty said.

"In the hustle of her departure, she forgot to pay our wages or give us extra money for food," Alfred added.

"I see," Cherry said, and unfortunately, she understood. Martinos's sister had left the mansion and her servants without a backward glance.

Bitch.

She was as nasty as Martinos had implied and cared nothing for her people, if she'd left them to these dire consequences. No obligation toward them. A search of the various rooms on the upper floors would confirm her theory.

She finished the last mouthful of a delicious fruit tart and drank the dregs of her surprisingly excellent tea. "Right. I'm going to satisfy my curiosity and explore the interior of the mansion." Cherry ignored Alfred's splutters and rose. "Tomorrow, I'll do a tour of the exterior."

"You can't do that," Alfred declared. "I'm the butler. You're nothing but a visitor and a human."

"Something isn't right. Don't you want to know if your Mistress is returning?"

"I don't wish to bother her," Alfred said.

"Alfred!" Betty stood and planted her hands on her hips. "Miss Cherry is right. No one lives in the mansion now. Apart from the dragon who dropped Miss Cherry here, we haven't seen another since those who left with Mistress Nandag. We can't continue as we have. Our food supplies are nil, and our money is low."

"You're not to wander around on your own. I'll go with you," Alfred said.

"We'll all go," Betty declared. "We must have answers."

Cherry led the procession from the kitchen, and this time she avoided the broken tile. "Which way first?"

"The bedrooms," Betty said. "I've never seen the bathtub or the shower that comes from the ceiling. They never allowed me on the upper floors."

"This is your chance to explore." If Cherry had her way, Betty and Alfred would move up to one of these bedrooms and use the running water. The more she learned of Nandag, the more she disliked the dragon woman. She was selfish, entitled, and an accessory to a crime.

"This is the first room." Alfred shunted the door open and stood aside for Betty and Cherry to enter.

Cherry walked straight to a wooden chest-of-drawers. She slid open the top drawer. Empty. Each of the other four held nothing but a red-and-black insect. The bug scuttled out, and Betty took a swift intake of breath, leaving Cherry to deal with the interloper.

"The wardrobe is empty too," Alfred said, after peering inside a wooden wardrobe with a carved door.

"Where are the blankets?" Cherry asked. "The bed linens?"

"Gone," Betty reported. "The chest at the end of the bed is empty. Only a small bag containing moth repellent herbs is left."

"We'll check the other bedrooms," Alfred said.

The three rifled through cupboards, drawers, and wardrobes. Each bore only insignificant items. Discarded objects no longer considered necessary.

"We'll check Mistress Nandag's chamber," Betty said in a tight voice.

Nandag's room was more luxurious and substantial than the others with an attached bathing chamber. Each of the cupboards and dressers was empty.

"How did you not notice?"

"Mistress Nandag had private servants who cared for her and any visitors. They left with the first wave of departures."

"What of the two servants who worked upstairs?"

Betty sniffed. "They're young and expect direction. I've had enough to do with cooking and cleaning. I'm not as young as I used to be."

Cherry stared at her. "But who have you been cooking for?"

"Mistress Nandag's parents. She moved them to a separate part of the estate. The old man was sick, and he drools. He's recovered somewhat, but he embarrassed her, so Mistress Nandag shifted them to the hunting lodge where she no longer had to see them."

"Right," Cherry said briskly. "Where are you sleeping?"

"We sleep on pallets in the kitchen," Alfred said.

"Pick a room and sleep on a mattress from now on," Cherry ordered. "I will pick a room too. There must be blankets elsewhere in storage or servants' rooms."

"We mustn't," Alfred said, aghast. "What if Mistress Nandag returns?"

Betty glared at her husband. "Do you think that likely, old man, when she has removed every personal possession and every single item of value from the public rooms? She never intended to return because that was never her plan. Our mistress didn't forget to pay us our wages. She duped us and cheated us out of our earnings."

"Please stop. You left Cherry on her own. What if Nandag is there? What if she hurts Cherry? You know our sister. She used to pull the wings off insects and injure small animals for her pleasure. She's older. Meaner. I saw her when she visited us in the dungeon. She has more control now, which only makes her more dangerous."

"No!"

It was the first time his dragon had spoken to him, and the single word punched emotion through Martinos. He was thrilled his dragon was not only alive, but he was healthy. But this wasn't the time to go rogue.

"Please."

"No!"

Martinos understood. Of course, he did. His dragon had spent three years bound. Imprisoned. Now that he had his freedom, he wished to enjoy every second, which meant flying—spreading his wings. How best to persuade his dragon to return to Smoking Isle? Because if he wasn't mistaken, the outline he could make out through the evening gloom and spits of rain was Perfume Isle.

He had expected his beast to falter due to exhaustion, but his dragon showed no signs of flagging.

Another dragon appeared without warning, flying on a direct path with him.

The dragon roared in a signal for Martinos to halt. The strident demand echoed through Martinos's head.

His dragon ignored the directive and continued on his journey, his pace not even slackening when a second and a third dragon appeared. Each of the dragons ordered him to acquiesce to their demands. It was easy to understand them without their words. *What did he want? Why was he entering their territory?*

His dragon continued to ignore the intense bombardment of summons.

"You will get us killed. At least answer their questions and give them our name. By Lodar! Cherry's safety depends on us, and we can't keep her safe if we're dead."

"I am Martinos of Smoking Isle," his dragon boomed, using the vocal pathway used by unrelated dragons.

Martinos held his breath as his dragon deigned to offer his identification. Now he had to pray the other dragons backed off and offered no obstruction to them passing through Perfume Isle territory.

"Martinos, The Rapist, what is your purpose?"

Martinos gasped, pain punching him hard in the gut on hearing the title the dragon used.

His dragon didn't hesitate this time. *"I seek news of what is happening at the castle on Hissing Isle."*

"Why?"

"I must plan," his dragon declared. *"I require information to do so."*

The approaching dragons remained silent. A family group, Martinos decided. With a common family channel. He prayed they'd have news. News to appease his dragon because concern for Cherry chafed him. His dragon had seized her and flown across the ocean. He'd flown high in the bitter cold. Worse of all, Cherry might face danger at the mansion. He'd witnessed the mean teasing the privileged dragons favored to amuse themselves.

"We will talk," one dragon announced. *"You may sup with us, and we will tell you all we have learned during the past days."*

"Thank you," his dragon returned, and Martinos relaxed. The dragons knew of the charges against him, yet had still invited him into their home. Luck was running his way. His dragon was right to request information.

The three dragons wheeled through the sky, and soon the crags and valleys of Perfume Isle were below them. The sweet scent of exotic spices and plants filled the air. Martinos had visited once before his parents had argued with the ruling family and had no longer been welcome. His dragon had taken a risk traveling here.

The buildings of a village appeared below them, and one by one, the dragons landed. His dragon followed suit and sat on his haunches, his breathing hard and choppy.

"You've overdone things," Martinos said. *"I warned you. After this time, you need to rebuild your strength, just as I have had to eat and regain muscle."*

"Nag," his dragon shot back.

Better than an abrupt no.

The dragons shifted to divulge, as Martinos had expected, members of the ruling family.

"We are searching for our sister," one of the men said. "Have you seen her?"

His dragon shook his head.

"Shift," the man ordered. "We wish to speak in human form."

His dragon ignored the order.

"We have vulnerable humans present. I cannot have you spraying fire or losing your temper. Shift, or you won't hear the news they bring with them. Recent and up-to-date news," the man added.

"You are no longer bound. Please acquiesce. Do not create trouble. I promise I will shift back to your form as soon as our discussions have ended. Please do not anger them."

His dragon appeared to consider Martinos's plea and finally yielded. Martinos's shift commenced and completed so fast he turned dizzy and stumbled.

"Why didn't you shift when we asked? What trickery is this?" the man demanded. He was a similar height to Martinos, but given his muscular bulk, he appeared in peak condition. His long, light brown hair stirred in the breeze while the expression in his stern features demanded answers.

"I apologize," Martinos murmured, bowing his head in deference. The two other dragons bore a similar appearance to the first, although both had lighter colored hair. "My dragon has been bound for three years and has only recently shifted. He seized control and refused to yield to me. It is only his desire for news that forced him to release the reins."

"Martinos," a feminine voice said from behind him. "Is that you? What are you doing here?"

"Gwenyth! Leo! You're safe. You escaped the soldiers."

Leo regarded him with his normal stoic expression of distrust. Gwenyth bore a bright smile of welcome and relief.

"I'm so glad. And your dragon is free now."

Gwenyth bounced in his direction and reached out her arms as if she thought to hug him.

Martinos took a rapid step back, not wanting to anger Leo. Newly mated dragons were possessive. After meeting Cherry, Martinos understood why.

Gwenyth stopped, and her brow furrowed. "What's wrong?"

"I don't wish to anger Leo." Martinos gestured at his lack of clothes. "It's not suitable form to hug, especially when I am not wearing clothes."

Leo released a loud growl, and one of the other dragons laughed.

"I will get clothes for us, and we will talk," a dragon said.

"Leo, you can make the introductions on my return." The dragon strode away and returned wearing trews and a matching black tunic. His clothes were plain and serviceable and did nothing to draw attention to his wealth. While Martinos hadn't met this dragon, he knew of him and the immense riches he and his family wielded. Over his arm, he carried three cloaks. He tossed one at Martinos, who hurriedly donned it before turning to Leo.

"I am glad you escaped the soldiers. You are both well?" Now that he had scrutinized Gwenyth, he noticed she held her body stiffly, and bandages covered her left arm.

"A little dinged-up during a battle with Nandag," Gwenyth said. "My true name is Liza Carrington. I lost my memory before I met you, but it has fully returned now."

"You fought Nandag?" he asked, replaying her words. Surely not?

"Your sister wasn't as smart as she thought." Gwenyth hesitated. "She's dead."

Martinos's brows rose, and he momentarily forgot what he'd intended to say. "You killed her?"

Liza pressed her lips together in a slight grimace. "Yes. I'm sorry."

Although he'd wanted the privilege, he realized it didn't matter. His sister couldn't bully, castigate, or punish anyone ever again. "No need to apologize, Gwenyth. I mean Liza. Cherry and your sister Rena will be excited to hear you're alive. They were worried about what they should tell your daughter."

"How do you know Cherry and Rena? Joanna." Liza speared him with her intense gaze. "You know my daughter? Where is she? Does Tony have her?" Her voice rose, panic taking her by storm, and she took half a step toward Martinos as if she wanted to shake the answers from him. "Tell me."

Leo wrapped his arm around her shoulders and cradled her against his side.

"Cherry and Rena hid Joanna," Martinos said. "Cherry picked Holy Island because it's closed off from visitors when the sea covers the causeway."

The largest of the brown-haired dragons spoke. "I am Blaze. These are my brothers, Rafael and Griffith. Come, we will have refreshments while we exchange information."

He led them into a cottage and gestured them to chairs. Meanwhile, Blaze's brothers produced bread, cheese, and a flask of wine and handed out tankards.

"What happened after we parted?" Leo asked. "Tell us everything."

Liza dragged a hand through her hair, disordering her locks. Her gaze was still intent, a little wild. "I can't believe this. How did you meet Cherry and Rena? Where? This is such a huge coincidence. I can scarcely believe it. Are you certain Joanna is safe from Tony?" Liza demanded. "You're not lying to us?"

"This is the honest truth. I promise, I would not lie to you, not after all you and Leo have done for me." Martinos smiled at his shared memories with Joanna and Cherry. "You have a charming daughter." He gestured at Leo. "I followed your suggestion to make for the human village. Your friends helped me. I met Sam and aided him to mend his nets while we waited for Henry to return from his fishing trip. Sam and his wife gave me clothes, a place to bathe and sleep, and a meal. The next day, Henry took me out on his fishing boat, and I worked as part of his crew."

"You?" Blaze asked. "Everything we heard of you indicated you were spoiled and lazy."

"I used to be a selfish, entitled landowner. The passing years have changed me, and I'm not too proud to work in exchange for help from others." Martinos paused, marshaling his thoughts. "The seas were rough on the day we sailed. We were traveling to one of Henry's fishing spots when a rogue wave struck us. It swept me overboard, and when I washed up, I was on Holy Island with no way of getting back to the Dragon Isles."

Blaze sat forward, his gaze intent. "Do you think you can go there again?"

"Possibly," Martinos said. "Cherry and Joanna found me on

the beach. Cherry took pity and offered me food and shelter. She helped me blend with the human world. Thanks to Cherry and Rena, I met with a druid who was able to conduct the required spell to free my bound dragon."

"Your arm bears a scar where the armband used to be," Liza said. "It looks painful."

Martinos shrugged, the movement pulling at the new scar and streaking discomfort down his arm. He bit his tongue and forced back the pain. It was an insignificant price to pay for his dragon's freedom. "My wounds will heal as I regain my strength."

Blaze leaned forward. "Leo and Liza told us what happened with your sister and how you and Liza escaped from the dungeon. Continue."

"Cherry and I spotted one of Leonidas's brothers walking through the human town on Holy Island. Nemyr, The Scary, noticed us and let us know he recognized me. We went for a drive and Cherry, Joanna, and I met with Rena and her druid. He performed the spell to free my dragon." Martinos slowed, then blurted the rest. "Once my dragon was unbound, he took control and seized Cherry. We flew through the barrier. My dragon released Cherry at my parents' mansion on Smoking Isle and flew here, seeking information. I hope Cherry is safe and well. At least my worry of Nandag approaching Cherry won't come to pass."

"So Rena is with my daughter?"

"Yes."

"Are Rena and Joanna in danger?"

"I pray not," Martinos said. "I'm hoping Nemyr focused on me rather than anyone else."

Liza bit her lip and exchanged a glance with Leo. "You're not sure."

"I'm sorry I can't give you certainty."

"Did you see any other dragons on the human side?" Blaze asked.

"No," Martinos said. A thought occurred. "How did you get here, Liza?"

"Leo went for a flight, and the barrier between our worlds had disappeared. He was flying along the coast. I was driving, and a dragon flew in front of my vehicle. Shocked the hell out of me, and I drove off the road. Leo rescued me before I drowned and flew through the barrier. It snapped back into place, trapping me here. Of course, I didn't understand what had happened because I'd hit my head and lost my memory. Leo and I are traveling to Smoking Isle, hoping to gain access to the druids."

"David, the druid I met with, asserts their world is in a state of upheaval. I'm not sure what is happening, but I suspect the druids in charge are allowing certain dragons to cross to the mainland."

Blaze refilled his tankard and offered more wine to Leo and Martinos. "That makes sense. They must open the protective barrier at certain times of the day. Sasha, our younger sister, flew to visit a friend and never returned. There is no reason for her disappearance. She promised to return for dinner and always keeps her word. Could she have flown through the barrier and become trapped on the other side?"

"Yes," Martinos said. "That is entirely possible."

Blaze frowned and glanced at his brothers. "Martinos has returned safely. Liza is safe after her journey through the barrier. We must trust in our little sister." His mouth twisted, and he barked out a single laugh. "She told us we kept her protected, and she'd never meet a mate with us looming a few steps behind her. Our parents had arranged a betrothal for her, and on the day she disappeared, she argued with my mother. Now she has her freedom and her chance to prove she is mature enough to live without our intervention."

"We'll find her," Leo said. "Now that we understand travel between the worlds is not an accident, but due to the druids' plan, we can devise our strategy."

Martinos glanced at Leo. "Where did Nandag catch you?"

"At the end of Hissing Isle, right before we reached the sea to fly to Perfume Isle." Liza reached over the table and slipped her hand in his. "I *am* sorry about Nandag."

Martinos gaped at her as she squeezed his hand in silent sympathy.

Leo freed Liza's hand from contact with Martinos and threaded his fingers with hers. "You had no choice. She was trying to kill you." He connected his gaze with Martinos's. "I killed my youngest brother, Goticranth, Eater of Bunnies, since he had aligned with your sister. He attacked me. In both cases, we either fought, or we died."

"Don't apologize because I'm not sorry," Martinos said. "She wasn't an affable dragon." *An understatement.* His sister had destroyed lives without the blink of an eye. "What news of your other brothers? Nemyr is traveling between our worlds. What of your oldest brother? Is he still alive?"

"Russays, The Magnificent," Leo said. "I didn't see him when Liza and I were at the castle."

"Me neither," Martinos said. "I'm not even positive he was part of the plot to imprison me."

Blaze set his tankard on the table with a definitive click. "We will treat him as hostile until we learn otherwise."

Everyone grunted assent.

Martinos relaxed. Now that his sister was dead, at least he could cease gazing over his shoulder. She couldn't injure Cherry.

"What's our next move?" Blaze asked.

"Set up a base on Smoking Isle and demand an audience with the head druid. While we're waiting, we can test the barrier and attempt to force our way through," Griffith suggested.

"What if you travel to the mainland?" Liza asked. "You need a plan for when you reach the other side. A base, so you don't attract unwanted attention. It's not usual for people in my world to see a dragon in full flight."

"Cherry's cottage," Martinos said. "I presume Rena will stay there with Joanna. We need Liza or Cherry or both to write letters for us to carry to introduce us to Rena."

Leo nodded approval. "A two-pronged attack. We should work in teams."

"That makes sense," Blaze said.

"I must return to Cherry," Martinos said. "I'm worried about her."

"Give us half an hour to plan, and we'll fly together," Blaze said. "It is safe to fly during the night. This way, we can start our plan on waking in the morn." He and his brothers left them alone.

Martinos nodded, even though urgency ate at him. *"Is that acceptable to you?"* he asked his dragon via their private communication channel. His dragon didn't reply, but he didn't force a shift either.

Martinos took that as assent.

Liza tapped him on the shoulder, and he started. He hadn't noticed her stand and round the table.

"Sorry," she said with a grimace. "Cherry is really here?"

"She is," Martinos said. "Your friend is a special lady."

She cocked her head, her eyes widening. He could practically read her thoughts as her lips tilted upward. "You like her."

"A lot," Martinos told Liza. "If Cherry agrees, I want her to become my mate. The problem is she wishes to stay on the mainland. She loves her bookstore, and I doubt she'll be happy anywhere else."

Liza grasped his wrist and squeezed. Excitement filled her face, and a smile bloomed, slow and sweet. "You truly understand her."

"I love her," Martinos said, unsure why he was admitting the truth to Liza when he hadn't spoken of his emotions to Cherry.

Liza's smile faded, and suspicion dimmed her exhilaration. "That was swift." Then she clapped her hand over her mouth, her eyes full of apology. "Cripes, sorry. That's hypocritical when my relationship with Leo was just as speedy."

"Our time together was full of danger. Everything happened fast, but that doesn't make my emotions toward Cherry less. I've never met a woman like Cherry." He paused. "Apart from you."

"Liza is mine," Leo interrupted. "We're married."

"You realize that on our side of the barrier, I'm still married to Tony."

Leo growled. "Not for long, if I ever get my hands on him."

Martinos nodded in total agreement. "The man deserves punishment for the way he has treated you and your daughter. I don't know how he could produce a daughter of such high caliber."

"Thank you," Liza said. "I can't wait for Leo and Joanna to meet each other. It will be great seeing Cherry again."

"Cherry missed you terribly. The police divers discovered your car, but they couldn't find you," Martinos said.

Blaze arrived with his two brothers. "I've given my subordinates instructions. We're ready to leave."

Martinos stepped away to give himself room to shift without injuring another dragon or Liza. He shrugged off the cloak and shifted.

"*You kept your word,*" his dragon said.

"*We are a team. Without the other, we are weaker. Together, we are strong.*"

Along with the other dragons, Martinos lifted into the air. This time, he breathed in the cold air and enjoyed the flight—the freedom of darting through the sky with the wind pressure against his wings and scaled body. The rest and the food and drink had revived his energy levels, but he suspected he'd sleep well this eve.

It was almost three hours later when they landed outside the mansion where he'd spent his childhood. The building lay in darkness with not a glimpse of light. Martinos frowned.

"Are you certain Cherry is still here?" Leo asked.

"I hope so," Martinos said. Although Cherry was safe from his sister, the other high-level dragons would pose a risk to her. With ground-eating steps, he raced up the steps and into the mansion via the main entrance. "Cherry!" he hollered. "Cherry, are you here? Cherry!"

"Who's there?" a belligerent male demanded.

"Martinos. Is Cherry here?"

"The red-haired wench," the man said. "Interfering busybody. Yes, she is here."

"Safe?"

"We are not barbarians," the man snapped.

"Where is Cherry?" Liza asked.

"Room at the top of the stairs." The man sniffed. "I suppose you wish food and accommodation."

"Go back to bed," Martinos said. "I will deal with my guests. We will find what we need."

"You what?"

An elderly woman appeared. "Come back to bed, husband. This is Cherry's young man. You'll find her upstairs, although she's probably awake with this racket. I'll leave the candlestick here so you can see what you're doing. You'll find cloaks in the cupboard to the right for those dragons who require one."

Martinos charged up the stairs, leaving the candlestick for his party.

Uncaring of his nudity, he wanted to see Cherry to assure himself she was unharmed by his dragon's actions.

"I didn't hurt her," his dragon said, sounding sulky.

"Wait until you meet her. I find her brave and courageous—a worthy partner for us."

"A mate?"

"If I have my way. I'm unsure how to win her since she'd prefer to live on the human side of the barrier. It would mean restrictions for us."

"No," his dragon snapped. *"I won't do it."*

Martinos ignored him, deciding to worry later. He crashed through the door, shoving it so hard it bashed against the wall.

Cherry sprang upright in the bed.

"Cherry. It's me. Martinos."

"Martinos!" She grinned. "About time you returned. We have much to discuss."

CHAPTER 14

The Reunion

Martinos sprang forward and dragged Cherry into his arms. He breathed in her familiar scent, the pain in his chest replaced with tingling warmth and a release of tension. "Are you unharmed?" He set her away an arm's length and did a rapid body scan. He saw no visible wounds. Martinos dragged her close again. "I'm so glad to see you. My dragon was panicky and running amok."

Cherry patted his shoulder, her reassurance easing his self-loathing and fear. Her warm smile brightened his day further.

"I have bruises, but otherwise, I'm healthy and fighting-fit. Did you know your sister moved herself and her friends out of the mansion and left the servants penniless? She didn't bother to inform them of her intentions or pay them. She just left. You need to speak to her, make her put things right," Cherry snapped.

"Nandag is dead."

"Alfred and Betty were left with nothing. Anxious and no way of buying food and—" She broke off to stare at him. "She what?"

"Liza killed her when Nandag attacked her."

"Liza..." Cherry's face turned slack, her eyes growing round. "Liza fought a dragon. Is she...is she still alive?"

"I'm here," Liza chirped from behind Martinos.

"Liza?" Cherry pushed away from Martinos and whirled, her hair swishing Martinos in the face. "Liza, you're alive!" She threw herself at her friend, clutched her shoulders, and started sobbing. "I thought you were dead, and I'd have to tell Joanna. For days I've been stressing over what to say."

"This is the woman who scolded me. I did not take in the details of her appearance then. I wanted to escape her yack-yack-yack, *"his* dragon said, his tone one of consideration. *"Pretty lady. Glorious red hair."*

"It's as fiery as is her passion. I knew you'd think her worthy." Martinos barely stopped himself from gloating. His dragon had always displayed an obstinate streak and required careful management.

"We shall see," his dragon replied.

"Tell me everything," Cherry said to Liza. "I shan't sleep until I hear of your adventures. How does one kill a dragon?"

The two women left the room, and Martinos trailed them, enjoying seeing his two favorite women chattering together. In the kitchen, Cherry set to making the tea. She issued instructions and, once he'd found clothes to wear, sent him outside to collect water. She ordered Leo to find more chairs, much to the amusement of the brothers from Perfume Isle.

"Do you want bread and jam to go with your tea? I'm afraid supplies are limited. Nandag left no funds for Alfred and Betty to replenish the stores."

"Yes, we'd enjoy bread and jam," Blaze said.

Martinos grinned as Cherry shoved the loaf of bread and a knife to Blaze. As he exited the kitchen door, she was issuing orders to the two younger brothers, giving them jobs too.

When Martinos arrived with a bucket of fresh water, Liza was busy telling Cherry about her arrival and her loss of memory. In return, Cherry informed her of Joanna, Rena, and her own adventures.

"Do we have a plan?" Cherry asked.

"We do," Leo informed her and repeated everything they'd decided to do.

"A solid strategy. We can make this our base, but we need money to buy supplies." Cherry narrowed her gaze on Martinos. "You must pay your staff."

Martinos nodded, agreeing. While in the past, Nandag's actions wouldn't have concerned him, his integration with humans had helped him to see other points of view. A beneficial skill to employ in his future. "How many staff are left?"

"Betty said a few of the junior girls help, but it's more when they have the urge rather than consistently."

"I'll have a chat with Betty," Martinos promised. "But I have no money either."

"I will give you a loan." Leo handed over a fistful of golden coins.

"Thank you," Martinos said, meaning it with every breath he took. "I will repay you as soon as I can."

The next day, it embarrassed him not to recognize the elderly couple who'd greeted them the previous night. His parents had never entered the kitchen or bothered with servants unless they provided inferior service. The blunt discussion he had with the couple told him as much and fueled his anger. Not that he let Betty and Alfred see his fury. None of this was their fault.

"This is for your wages." He shunted a pile of gold coins toward the couple. "One of my friends has offered to organize running water for the kitchen and to the washhouse."

"No more toting heavy buckets from the well," Betty said, beaming in satisfaction. "Thank you, sir."

"Call me Martinos," he said. "If you have any problems, come and find me, or let Cherry or one of the others know. We'll work out a way to solve them. Hire more staff as you need them."

"More staff?" Alfred asked.

"Or if I can help with a task, ask me."

"You, sir?" Betty asked, her face slack with shock.

"Martinos," he prompted with a smile. "Yes, I enjoy working with my hands and learning unfamiliar tasks."

"If I make a list of supplies, c-can you procure them from the market? Alfred and I find the walk exhausting."

"Consult with Cherry while I visit my parents," Martinos said. "I will return in an hour to collect your list." He smiled at the flabbergasted couple and departed. He found Cherry loitering at the kitchen exit, and a broad smile broke over her face when she spotted him.

"Well done."

"I meant every word."

"I know you did," she said. "Can I visit your parents with you?"

Martinos hesitated. "My parents are not pleasant. They will treat you with scorn because you are a human."

Cherry sniffed. "I don't care what they think of me. It's your opinion that matters."

His dragon made a soft sound of wonderment, and Martinos's chest expanded with a wealth of emotions that were too tangled for him to comprehend right now. This woman. "I love you, Cherry."

She beamed before her face fell. "What are we going to do, Martinos? Our worlds are so different. I want to return to the mainland. I adore my bookstore, but I don't want to lose you either. No one has ever understood me the way you do."

"We will work things out. I promise."

Cherry sniffed, and her jaw clenched. "I don't see how."

"We might come from different worlds, but we found each other. Have belief, my sunbeam. We direct our paths with our determination and strength of character. I love you, and your courage was the first thing to attract me."

"Aw, tug on the heartstrings," his dragon taunted.

Martinos ignored the sly dig, pleased his dragon was communicating with him more often. "We need to fly to get to where my parents are living at present."

"How long will the flight take?"

"Ten to fifteen minutes," Martinos said. "Flying is the best way to travel. A journey through the mountains will take several hours."

"We fly," Cherry said. "Let me find more clothes to help me keep warm. I'll meet you out front in a few minutes."

His dragon crouched while Cherry scrambled onto his back, taking a position between the ridges that grew along his spine. Her thighs gripped his scales, and her small hands grasped a sharp fold on his back in the way Leo and Liza had demonstrated. Once she was secure, they took off and rapidly gained in height. From high above, it was possible to see the crater of the main volcano. A lake filled the depression, and today, the smoke coming off the lake was minimal, making for an impressive view.

With powerful wing strokes, his dragon soared through the sky.

"I wish the flight was longer. I dreamed of flying free and soaring over the mountains of our home."

"Would you ever wish to leave?" Martinos asked his dragon, this conversation bringing satisfaction and pleasure. Connecting with his dragon amplified his senses and completed him. It was a bubbling, heady sensation, one he'd never take for granted again.

"Depends," his dragon responded after an interminable silence. *"If I could still fly and embrace my dragon side. Our sister has left a mess at the mansion. I don't understand her plan, but she had a strategy."*

"She was determined to go ahead with her betrothal to Leo. I've never understood this since Leo is the youngest son. Why not marry the oldest who stands to inherit?"

"Exactly," his dragon said. *"Power is the best motivation. It gives one a position of strength."*

"Agreed. We had what I thought was a pleasant life here, but Nandag and my parents have left nothing of value. She took her trusted staff and friends with her. Gwenyth—I mean Liza—told me a small group arrived with Nandag. Where are the others?"

"Perhaps they are with our parents."

"We'll soon find out," Martinos said as his dragon soared lower and landed in front of the hunting lodge. As a child, Martinos had spent summers here, and his memories raised a smile. His dragon landed with care and lowered his body for Cherry to slither to the ground. Once he assured himself of her safety and she'd retreated,

he shifted forms.

"It's silent," Cherry commented. "The scenery is gorgeous."

Martinos glanced around the clearing where the lodge sat. Nothing stirred. Not a single human or dragon exited the place to welcome them or ask their business.

"Interesting." Martinos dressed and held out his hand. "Let's find my parents."

Cherry clasped Martinos's fingers and wandered at his side. They entered a low, squat building. The door hung awkwardly and scraped the floor when Martinos pushed it. A symptom shared by the rest of the structure. To Cherry's eye, the building had decent bones, but passing time and a lack of maintenance had taken their toll. An empty, unloved air wrapped around the property, and the interior radiated the same deserted impression with musty mildew assaulting her nostrils. Grimy windows filtered out the light.

Cherry advanced with caution but still walked into a spiderweb. She brushed at her face, the hair at the back of her neck standing to attention. Her gaze darted through the shadows. "Where is everyone?"

"I don't know. We'll search room-by-room."

Cherry followed Martinos, part fascinated and part horrified at the dragon world. The dragons lived like feudal lords and cared little for those below them in rank. They hadn't moved on but continued to dwell in the past. Arriving here had been the equivalent of walking into a Middle Ages storybook. No wonder the mod-cons had thrown Martinos when he ended up in her world. He'd adjusted well. She frowned, recalling Liza's future intentions. She'd told Cherry she and Leo had married in a church, and even though Tony was her lawful husband, she'd stay with Leo. She planned to recover Joanna and return to the Dragon Isles, where she was out of Tony's reach.

The ultimate disappearance act.

Liza had mentioned Leo's farm and his gorgeous cabin that had running warm water and toilet facilities. It was cozy, and she and Leo couldn't wait to return there. His family was a problem to that outcome, or so Liza had informed her.

Martinos opened yet another door, and a sickroom stench wafted out, slapping them in the face. They halted to allow their gazes to adjust to the dim light.

"Father," Martinos said.

"Mart...Martinos?"

"Yes."

"Thought you dead. N-Nandag said—"

Martinos cut in, imagining only too well the lies his sister had spread. "Where is everyone?"

"Gone," the rail-thin man, lying on the bed, croaked. "Dead."

"How?"

"Thought a disease came from the human village. L-last dragon standing."

Cherry gripped Martinos's arm in case he had ideas of going closer. His father's skin was bright red—not a sunburned ruddy, but a splotchy, uneven scarlet. One half of his face was lower than the other.

"D-don't worry," the wizened man said. He coughed and spat out a chunk of phlegm, uncaring when it landed on his bedcovers. "Others died...weeks ago. I am old, tired. Without food."

"You're coughing up red phlegm," Cherry said. "That's not normal."

"Ah," the man said, breathless with the effort of speaking. "Mayhap I will pass soon and travel beyond this misery."

"You blamed the humans? Why?" Cherry asked.

"Excellent point," Martinos said.

The man scrunched his brow. "T-thought they caused...this. Humans started dying."

"Who proposed they were to blame?" Martinos asked.

"Your sister."

"She left, knowing you were sick?"

Cherry heard Martinos's anger at his sister's lack of compassion and her need to put herself before others.

"Is it possible this isn't a disease?" Cherry whispered. "Would your sister and those who follow her stoop to poison? Look at your father's color. It's not normal."

"Father, could you have eaten or drunk poison?"

The elderly dragon didn't speak for long moments. Cherry

wondered if he'd gone to sleep or, worse, died.

"Nandag brought us twenty cases of expensive wine," his father said finally. "We had so much we shared a bottle or two with the servants. It was around that time the first deaths occurred. The humans died while Nandag was still visiting. She laughed and called them weak." His brow furrowed, and he coughed. Once. Twice. Three times. More red phlegm exploded from his mouth.

"Do you have any wine left?"

"I am drinking the last bottle. When I became too weak to raise the bucket from the well, I drank wine instead."

"Where are the dead?" Martinos asked.

"I buried them one by one until I no longer had the strength to dig holes."

"What did you do then?" Cherry asked.

"I left the bodies for the wild animals."

Cherry swallowed hard. "If Nandag poisoned the wine, your sister's actions do not speak well for her." She turned to Martinos's father. "Nandag is dead. She died while trying to murder my friend."

"I see." He coughed. "She ran our business to extract maximum profit. Workers left because she ceased paying them. Output fell, and the quality of the finished product deteriorated. Sales slowed. T-tried to tell her. She laughed, told me I knew nothing. She informed me the business was producing products for the luxury market, creations to maintain family pride."

"She forgot humans and dragons of a lower class purchased our plates and utensils," Martinos said with a snort. "I might've been a spoiled son who took my privilege for granted, but I understood business—our trade and how it worked." He turned to Cherry. "I never helped much in the production. At first, I was too busy playing, and then when I was ready to step in, I faced rape charges."

Cherry glimpsed the distaste on his father's face and spoke in his defense. "Martinos was innocent. Your daughter and her friends manipulated the charges. I believe it was to get rid of Martinos to further her plan, whatever that was."

"Nandag did this?" The elderly man coughed, a wet, rattling gurgle. "Then I have wronged you, my son. Nan became angry when she discovered I had kept funds aside. I hid family treasure, and she couldn't sniff it out. It was after that argument she brought us the wine." He laughed weakly, and his coughing started again. "The wine contained poison. I now know this as fact."

Martinos stepped forward and helped his father to sit. "Why did you continue to drink it if you suspected poison?"

"Already sick. T-too weak to get to the well. The wine has a w-wonderful flavor. Decided to use it to ease my thirst. I am old. Dispirited. Close friends have died, thanks to my daughter." He heaved a sigh and coughed, his thin shoulders shaking. "At least it is almost gone. I'd hate more people to die. People who depend on us require work and direction."

She and Martinos leaned closer to hear his hoarse words and

hopefully an explanation.

"What people?" Cherry asked. "Only Betty and Alfred remain at the mansion. They have little help from the village."

The elderly man puckered his brow. "No residents?"

"No."

"We haven't checked the village yet," Martinos said. "Perhaps they are there."

"The nobles?"

"We presume they journeyed with Nandag to Hissing Isle when she traveled to formalize her betrothal," Cherry said.

"I don't understand." Martinos's father coughed yet again, the rattle extending to his chest.

"We should get you to a doctor," Cherry murmured.

"No, do not waste the saw-bone's time. Not long left now. K-know signs."

"We can't leave you here alone," Cherry protested.

"Cherry is right. We will stay with you. Can we get you anything?"

"I am cold," his father said, and no sooner had he said the words than a shudder racked his body.

"We will find blankets," Cherry promised.

She and Martinos made a rapid search of the other bedrooms. Each was empty, and many stunk of bodily functions. Cherry opened the windows and searched the wardrobes for blankets. She located two woolen shawls in a chest and figured they'd work.

Once she'd covered him, she filled a bowl with warm water and washed his face to make him more comfortable.

"You're a kind woman," the elderly man managed between coughs.

"It's no trouble."

"Most of my acquaintances declined to stir themselves for fear of catching the disease. Then they died too because they drank the wine."

"Are you positive it was the wine?"

"I am," he said. "Nandag left a gloating note at the bottom of the case. It was I who discovered the message when I retrieved the last bottle. Too late to save anyone, I fear."

"Bitch," Cherry muttered.

The man barked out a weak laugh. "You have the right of it."

During the next few hours they sat with his father. He talked, so they listened and learned.

He died four hours later.

She and Martinos buried him, then removed and carted the soiled linens outside to burn. With the essential chores done, they closed up the hunting lodge and flew back to the mansion.

Leo and Liza plus Blaze and his brothers returned from their scouting missions, and once everyone was back, they shared information.

"My parents and their friends and staff at the hunting lodge are dead. Nandag gave them a gift of poisoned wine. Nobody realized the wine caused the mysterious deaths until my father, who was the last left alive, discovered Nan's note at the bottom of a crate."

Blaze whistled, the burst of air between his teeth an echo of the shock on all their faces. "That's cold."

"Yes." Martinos sighed. "Evidently, my father refused to give her the treasure he'd hidden. I wish I understood Nandag's plan."

"I want to kill her all over again," Liza spat. "Heartless bitch."

"My lodestone, thanks to you, I had a lucky escape," Leo said. "If it wasn't for meeting you, the pressure from my parents and older brothers to go ahead with the betrothal might have gotten to me. Nandag might've killed me next."

"No, not you," Liza said. "You would've told them to go to hell. Eventually."

"The village isn't as busy as I'd expect," Blaze said. "Most of the humans I spotted were older."

"The farmers have left their stock to roam and fend for themselves. None of the small businesses are operating," Rafael said. "I presume your island works on similar lines to ours?"

Cherry shared a glance with Martinos and witnessed his puzzlement.

"None of this makes sense," Martinos muttered. "I don't

understand Nandag's scheme."

"Leo and I visited the druids. We acted as if we wished to tour the gardens and enjoy the serenity. I hadn't expected such tight security. The druid on the gate made us wait until the head druid could greet us. I don't think it was my imagination, but I believe our arrival made him nervous," Liza said.

"Definitely," Leo said. "He hustled us around the garden and kept us away from the druid's quarters. I noticed they were building a new structure, but he didn't show us that area."

"A night time reconnoiter?" Cherry asked.

"Yes," Blaze said. "This puzzle intrigues me."

"Did anyone test the protective barrier?"

Blaze gestured at Griffith. "We did a flight out over the North Sea, but the barrier is intact."

"I had a thought," Cherry said. "Could the drop in the barrier coincide with the tide allowing vehicles to cross the causeway to Holy Island?"

"Those were the times we spotted Nemyr," Martinos said, his tone thoughtful.

"That could be it," Liza said with excitement. "Can you remember when the low tide is?"

"I can make a guess," Cherry said. "Does time pass in the same way here? I mean, if it is six here, will it be six on Holy Island?"

"No," Martinos said. "I believe time goes faster here. More things have occurred here and over many days."

"We saw Nemyr right before we visited the yew grove. How many hours have we been here? Almost twenty-two? Yes," Cherry confirmed her reasoning with a definitive nod. "We should try the barrier as soon as it's light."

"Right," Leo said. "Let's leave at sunrise."

Liza bounded to her feet. "I'm going with you."

Cherry rose. "Me too. It might be a chance for us to return."

Blaze scowled at his brothers. "Only one of us should go to search for Sasha."

The brothers shared a glance, using their familial line to communicate telepathically.

"I'll go," Blaze said, standing. "Let's grab a couple of hours of sleep, then attempt to cross the barrier."

CHAPTER 15

The Best-Laid Plans

"**W**hy are you scowling?" Martinos asked, coming up behind Cherry and tugging her against his chest.

"If we can get through, we'll separate. I'll travel home where I'll be alone. Liza is returning to Dragon Isles with Leo and Joanna. Rena is determined to spend time with David. You're set on departing for Smoking Isle."

Martinos tugged her around to see her face. He cupped her jaw, his expression tender yet concerned too. "Come with me."

Cherry frowned. "I've worked hard to grow my business. I love my books, and I'd miss my familiar world. My routine. Your world is different—rawer—with none of the things we take for granted."

Cherry pulled a face. "Popsicles, I sound self-centered and selfish. That's not what I mean. I'm torn. No matter what my decision, I'll lose part of myself."

"No, you're giving me the truth instead of what you think I want to hear. After the lies and scheming from my sister, I value honesty." Martinos pushed a curl off her face, his gaze searching. Determined. "Cherry, we're perfect together."

"She's our mate," his dragon stated emphatically. *"I feel it. I find myself craving her smile, her goodness. Our sunbeam helped us to escape our armband prison. Once I regained my senses, she charmed me as she has you. We can't let her leave."*

"My dragon craves you. We agree—my dragon and I. You're our woman. Our mate."

"I love you," Cherry said in a small voice.

"Then, we'll devise a plan to stay together," Martinos said. "Could you move your bookstore? To Holy Island or if the island won't produce enough income, maybe the nearby town we visited? At least that way, you'd live closer to Liza and Rena, and it might be possible to visit your friends. We'd see each other."

Cherry brightened. "I could do that. Remember the bookshop we saw when we visited the town? That might work if it's still for sale." Her mouth stretched in a broad smile, and excitement replaced her despondency. "Marvelous idea. It never occurred to me to use this as an opportunity instead of the end. Maybe we can do this because I'd miss Liza and Rena as well as you."

"What about your mother? Your customers? You'd have to rebuild your contacts."

"What are you doing, numbskull?" his dragon shrieked. *"You'd persuaded her. Now you're undoing your excellent maneuvering."*

Cherry lifted her hand in a wave of dismissal. "My mother is an independent soul, and since she always tells me I'm too conservative and need to spread my wings, she can hardly complain if I move to another town. I could visit the bookstore and check it out once we get to the mainland."

"Phew!" his dragon said. *"She's still considering a move closer. This might work."*

"Told you," Martinos said, so relieved his gamble had worked, his hands shook. He screwed them into fists and hid them behind his back.

Liza had wandered over to them while they were talking. "I couldn't help but overhear. Cherry, a move is a brilliant idea. You've wanted to expand but haven't had space. If you had a shop closer to Holy Island, it might be an idea to set up a base for the dragons who come to the mainland. You could act as a help center. It might turn into an extra stream of income for you."

"I could do that," Cherry agreed. "Although I'm not sure if I could afford to buy a large enough house or cottage to house visitors."

"Liza and I can help with funds," Leo said. "Money won't be a problem."

"Has anyone thought if dragons are finding their way through the barrier, then more humans will end up in your world?" Liza asked. "I worry over these changes. Most humans aren't ready to accept dragons are real."

"David is trying to learn what is happening at the monastery," Cherry said. "David believes we must control entry between the worlds. Dragons retreated to the isles for a reason. Spotting a dragon *will* terrify humans. They'll call out the army and the air force. Dragons wouldn't have a show against fighter planes. A panicked human is unpredictable."

"True." Liza scowled. "The heads of governments will attack with modern weapons or worse, the science community will covet the opportunity to capture and study a dragon for research. Then there are the druids. If the public learns their magic is real, the same problems come into play. The world isn't ready to learn dragons and druids are a thing."

"I hate to say it, but Liza is right," Cherry said. "We must restrict travel between the worlds to dragons and humans who understand the consequences. There should be repercussions if anyone flouts the rules."

"I agree," Liza said. "Once things settle, you'll have to approach the heads of government from each isle and work out how to manage the barrier. You might even decide you want the barrier full stop with no travel between Holy Island and the Dragon Isles." She glanced at the dragon males. "Do you agree with what we're saying?"

"The two of you understand your mainland world," Martinos said. "We'll let you guide us."

Leo and Blaze inclined their heads in assent.

"Should we patrol our sea borders in case humans enter our territory in error?"

"What if we asked Rena's druid to beef up the spell or whatever is there already to repel humans from the mainland side?" Liza asked. "Something to give a sense of dread if a human continues in his or her boat. Or maybe rough weather and immense seas around the barrier. I mean, the druids must've placed something to repel humans."

"Ask David when we see him next," Martinos said. "We can't have humans entering our world unrestricted. It will upset the balance."

Cherry nodded. "We'll do that as soon as we can."

"I wish to search for my sister," Blaze said. "Where should I start?"

"I suggest between Holy Island and where I drove into the ocean. Cherry and I can show you a possible search region once we reach the other side."

"My thanks," Blaze said. "And on that note, I'm grabbing a few winks of sleep."

"I'll wake everyone in time to leave," Leo said. He led Liza from the salon, in the same direction, Blaze had disappeared.

Martinos shunted her from the salon. "Come, sunbeam. We should rest."

She walked with Martinos to their chamber. Once the door closed behind them, she sat on the corner of the four-poster bed and smiled. "Make love to me. Please."

He crossed to her and took her into his arms. Seconds later, their lips met in a passionate kiss. Between kisses, their clothes melted away.

"I love you," he whispered. "We will make this work, I promise. If it weren't for the promise I'd made to my father, I'd stay on Holy Island instead of returning to Smoking Isle. Once I've completed my tasks, I promise to join you."

"You'd give up everything for me?" Her hands wandered his warm chest, and her eyes widened on spotting his dragon tattoo. She brushed her finger over Martinos's skin and the tattoo arched beneath her touch. "Wow." Cherry repeated her caress, and the dragon tattoo blew her a saucy kiss. "That's amazing. I'm so glad you and your dragon are united again."

"So am I, but back to our conversation before my dragon started flirting with you. I won't be losing a thing," Martinos said. "I'm gaining friends and a woman who is perfect for my dragon and me."

Together, they fell to the bed, arms wrapped around each other. Martinos stroked her arms, her back, her bottom, and her breasts until she quivered with need. He parted her legs with his thigh, and she groaned as he filled her. They rocked together, kissing and murmuring encouragement to each other. The pleasure grew, fast and furious, and Cherry surrendered to the passion, secure in the arms of her lover. She exploded, stars bursting behind her closed eyes.

Martinos used her mouth to smother his groan when his climax took him, his heart pounding against her chest. A distinct click sounded, ringing within her head. *Eek!* Her bones were cracking and creaking from overuse.

"I love you," Cherry whispered, every part of her in tune with this remarkable man. Dragon. "I'm so happy."

"He-haw! We have a true mate!"

Cherry gripped his shoulders, glancing around the shadowed chamber. "Who said that?"

"My dragon," Martinos said with a chuckle. "This is wonderful. He has accepted you as our mate. Our making love now that my dragon is free has cemented the bond. Even better, you should be able to communicate with us telepathically now."

Cherry relaxed a fraction. "Really?"

"Try it," he whispered. "Say hello to my dragon."

"Hello?" Cherry thought the words, unconvinced, despite Martinos's certainty. *"Um, are you there?"*

"Greetings, sunbeam. You are exquisite. Your red hair dazzles me." Martinos's dragon spoke with a deeper, grittier voice.

"What should I call you?"

"We are both Martinos." Martinos's voice sounded within her mind.

"Can I talk to you any time I want?" she asked, forgetting to speak with her thoughts.

"If we're in the same vicinity." his dragon answered the question. *"When we are on Smoking Isle, and you are not, we cannot communicate. It is not ideal."*

"I'm sorry," Cherry whispered.

"We will not be apart for long. I promise both of you this," Martinos said.

"Thank you," his dragon said, sounding repentant. *"I'm cranky because I don't wish us to part."*

"We have our tasks," Cherry said. "I'll try to help Blaze with his search for his sister."

"That is a generous thing to do," his dragon said. *"We will work to fulfill our promise. Many have suffered from Nandag's actions. We must make this right and help the residents of Smoking Isle to prosper."*

"You are an honorable dragon," Cherry said with pride. One who considered others, and the man she wished to have at her side. "The day I discovered you on the beach, my luck changed."

"No," his dragon said. *"We are the fortunate ones. Few dragons find their true mates."*

"That is correct. Until I met Leo and Liza, I believed fated mates were a myth," Martinos said. "No longer. The mate bond clicked into place, which means we have a future together, despite our paths separating us."

"A brief separation," Cherry said. "I intend to fight for us."

"As do I," his dragon declared.

"We are of one accord then," Martinos whispered. "Sleep, my mate. Rest and recuperate for our crossing. Our future together will come soon. I promise."

Each flight became more natural, and despite the darkness surrounding them, Cherry clutched the bag carrying men's clothes to her chest and searched the sky, seeking...she wasn't sure what. Leo and Martinos flew a determined path out to sea. Blaze kept pace with them. In the faint darkness, a few stars were still visible. The moon, which was three-quarters full, glinted over the sea. Cherry would've enjoyed the flight if it weren't for the intense cold.

Abruptly, the air thickened, dragging against her face and limbs. Martinos's progress slowed even though his wing-beats increased. He strained, exerting considerable energy, and without warning he shot forward with slingshot speed and bounced back.

Leo and Blaze slammed into the barrier too. Liza managed to retain her seat after the collision.

Cherry slid, almost losing her grip of Martinos's back ridges.

She overcorrected and lurched to the other side. This time she was unable to keep her balance. A second later, she was in freefall, her frantic scream clawing from her throat.

"Martinos!" *God, she'd never survive the fall.*

Cherry heard a faint scream from Liza, her friend's horror and panic clear.

"Martinos will get her," Leo said, and his words rang with positivity across the common channel.

How? They'd been flying so high, and she was falling rapidly. Whenever she'd flown, either on a plane or recently, with Martinos, the clouds had reminded her of giant puffs of cotton wool. Not true. They were wet and creepy when one was falling through them.

She dropped through another cloud and her clothes became sodden. Water dripped off the end of her nose, and still she kept falling. Fast. *So fast.*

"I'm coming, sunbeam."

As his calm words filled her mind, Martinos arrowed past her at speed, disappearing into the same cloud gloom that had swallowed her. Long seconds passed when she saw nothing. The speed of her fall had her hair whipping wildly around her face.

The cloud cover cleared and terror and dread forced a croak up her throat. Her fall was swift, and now she was close enough to the sea to spot the wave's whitecaps.

A flash of red shot before her and then Martinos was there. One big talon snapped out and curled around her, angling their fall into a more controlled arc.

Cherry's heart beat so fast she feared it might jump right out of her chest.

"Got you, sunbeam," Martinos whispered. *"You gave me a scare."*

"I scared the crap out of myself," Cherry muttered, her heart still bounding like a startled rabbit against the wall of her chest.

"We will always catch you should you ever fall," Martinos's dragon stated. *"We will always be there for you."*

"My dragon speaks true. We love you and will support you in every way possible. You are our other half."

A lump grew in Cherry's throat, and she coughed to clear it. No one had ever wanted her or cared for her happiness and wellbeing in this way. *"Thank you,"* Cherry said. *"I don't know what I did to deserve you."*

"My grandmother would have said it was kismet," Martinos declared.

"Do you believe in fate?"

"I do now."

Cherry heard the grin in his tone, his happiness and satisfaction. *"At least you didn't try to tell me I fell for you."*

"I would never," Martinos said.

"Haw-haw. I wish I'd thought of telling Cherry that," his dragon said. *"She did fall."*

"Don't remind me," Cherry said. *"My life passed in front of my*

eyes."

They burst through a cloud to find Blaze and Leo swooping toward them.

"Cherry, are you all right?" Liza demanded. "I never want to experience fear like that again."

"I can hear Liza," Cherry said. "Should I hear her?"

"Cherry?" Liza's voice reverberated in Cherry's head. "You and Martinos are mates!"

"Yes," Martinos's dragon crooned, sounding supremely happy. "Congratulate us. We are official."

"We have our personal channel and another we use to communicate with other dragons," Martinos informed her. "Our dragon switched channels for us."

"Oh, Liza. I think my life passed in front of my eyes. Thank goodness Martinos caught me in time." Thank destiny! Her breathing was still choppy at the idea of striking the water after falling from such a great height. "What do we do now? If we can't cross the barrier, I mean."

"We search for another way," Martinos said.

"Which way?" his dragon asked. "I was not wholly functional during the last time we flew over this region of Smoking Isle."

"We might as well fly over the monastery," Leo said.

Martinos wheeled in the direction Leo had suggested, and Blaze followed. Ten minutes later, the three dragons landed and shifted. Cherry and Liza handed them clothes from the bags they'd strapped to their backs.

"I hope you have a plan B and C," Blaze said. "How the hell did my sister get through the barrier? If that's where she is. Damn, the not knowing is upsetting my entire family."

A shrill call cut through the silence of the night and the murmur of their voices.

"Nemyr," Leo said in a grim voice. "And a backup."

It was Zephyr, one of Nandag's followers. Rage exploded through Martinos, fueled in part by his dragon. *"I must punish Nemyr and Zephyr,"* his dragon shouted. *"Attack!"*

"We can't leave Liza and Cherry without protection," Martinos protested as Leo yanked off his clothes again.

"I'll stay with the women," Blaze said. "I will protect them as if they were my sisters."

Martinos shifted, and his dragon bowed his head to Blaze in a show of respect and thanks. Then he took to the air, narrowly missing Nemyr's extended talons.

Martinos wasn't as strong as usual, but determination lent him tenacity. His fury. His disgust. His urgent need to protect Cherry all worked in his favor.

"Our mate," his dragon declared.

Joy spread through Martinos before he went into a rapid dive. He and Nemyr collided in mid-air. Talons ripped, and teeth slashed while their whipping wings maintained their hover. Zephyr attacked from behind, gouging Martinos's knobby spine.

An instant later, the pressure disappeared from his back, and Leo's battle cry echoed through the skies.

Martinos doubled down, but the time his dragon had spent in exile had taken their toll. He required longer to recover.

Nemyr roared in a challenge, his eyes gleaming red as he charged.

"Pretend we're wounded," Martinos told his dragon. *"Let him think he has us beat. We need to time this right. Dart out of the way and rip open his chest. We don't have the energy to continue beating him back."*

"Plan," his dragon replied and set their strategy into action.

He faltered when Nemyr charged. His wing-beats slowed, and he issued a distressed roar. Nemyr's bugle was loud and triumphant.

"Idjit," his dragon scoffed.

"Don't get overconfident," Martinos warned. *"We cannot fail. This is our first and last opportunity."*

Nemyr extended his talons and roared, his fury emerging in flames. Martinos avoided a collision at the last second. He darted to the side and charged before Nemyr turned his more muscular body. Martinos blew his flames in Nemyr's face, obscuring his vision and singeing his face. The stench of burning flesh filled Martinos's nostrils as he and his dragon launched a quick, furtive attack. He raked his claws over Nemyr's vulnerable chest. Made contact. When Martinos dragged his talons free, blood spurted from the wound he'd inflicted.

Nemyr issued a furious bellow. His wing strokes faltered, and Martinos reached for extra energy. His dragon was lagging.

"Attack. Attack again while he's still in shock from our blow."

His dragon flew, but sluggishly now.

"One more attack, and we'll have him."

"You are nothing," Nemyr screamed at him. *"A useless son with no vision. Nandag is the brains in your family and worth more than you. You are nothing."*

"Interesting," his dragon said.

"He doesn't know Nandag is dead. They're working together, but each has their own responsibilities," Martinos replied.

Nemyr charged, fury turning him careless.

Martinos ripped a second, deeper hole in Nemyr's chest. Nemyr faltered, his ragged breaths bubbling in a death rattle. He shuddered, and when he summoned his fire, smoked poured from the wound in Nemyr's chest.

"Once more," Martinos urged his dragon. *"One more charge. Do we have the energy?"*

"Yes!"

His dragon rallied, but Martinos worried at his fatigue, the sluggish maneuvering.

"We can do this. We must to save Cherry."

Grit flooded Martinos, he and his dragon united in their need to protect their mate.

He and Nemyr collided again.

"I will win," Nemyr boasted, still arrogant and confident of his abilities despite the rattle in his throat.

"No, he won't," Martinos told his dragon.

They wheeled through the sky, willpower and resolve lending them strength, bolstering their endurance. This time the two dragons clashed head-on, and the impact of their collision echoed like a clap of thunder. Martinos internalized the pain and raked his claws across Nemyr's chest.

Nemyr released a startled gurgle. For an instant, he hovered, his expression incredulous. Seconds later, he fell. He splashed into the sea and sank.

Martinos watched until Nemyr disappeared and waited to ascertain he didn't reappear. Reassured of Nemyr's death, Martinos turned to check on Leo's progress. Leo attacked ceaselessly, not allowing Zephyr to rally.

It was an honor to watch Leo, Champion of the Skies, in action.

"He is a talent," his dragon said.

"We should ask him to help us regain our fitness," Martinos said.

When his dragon didn't protest, Martinos made a mental note to ask Leo for help.

"We can protect Cherry if we are stronger," his dragon said.

"Our mate," Martinos said.

He had much to consider—plans to make for their future.

"We'll woo her," his dragon declared. *"If we take her flowers. Give her a sweet-tart to tempt her. Sing her a song she might change her*

mind and stay with us."

"What? No! No singing. If we sing, we'll scare her away. Not that it matters at present. None of us are crossing the barrier."

Zephyr bellowed, turned tail and fled. Blood leaked from a wound on his flank, and a second gash gaped open near the base of his tail. Leo gave chase and Martinos followed. Zephyr retreated faster than Martinos would've expected. Suddenly, Zephyr came to an abrupt halt. He fell, plummeting into the sea.

The pair slowed to hover in the air and watched for Zephyr's reappearance. When it didn't happen, they glided back to rejoin Blaze and the women standing on the beach.

Martinos landed and shifted, his transformation more sluggish than usual.

Cherry ran to his side. "Are you injured?"

"A few cuts and scratches," he said, cataloging his lacerations. "Nothing major. I will heal. It was a pleasure to watch you fight," he told Leo once he'd shifted. "I wondered if you'd help me to train and regain my fitness."

"I exercise most days. You're welcome to join me." Leo accepted a pair of trousers from Liza and pulled them on to cover his nakedness.

"Talk later, boys. If we can't get through the barrier, we'll need to return to Martinos's home." Liza linked arms with Cherry.

Cherry wrinkled her nose, and Martinos smiled at the cute habit. During the fight, dawn had approached on this side of the barrier.

"It's a pity we couldn't interrogate Nemyr and Zephyr," Leo murmured.

"Aye," Blaze said. "We still have no inkling what they were up to on Holy Island."

"The druid's behavior when Liza and I visited the monastery inspired suspicion. I believe they—or at least some of those at the monastery—are part of whatever scheme Nandag, Nemyr, and Goticranth were—are—up to," Leo said. "I believe that is our next avenue to explore."

"That's our plan, then," Cherry said. "We fly to the monastery and speak with the head druid, although it might show our hand. Maybe we should sneak into the monastery and discover what we can."

"Our Cherry," his dragon purred in approval.

"Credit me with finding her first," Martinos teased, glad he and his dragon were one when it came to their sunbeam.

"She thinks she is weak, but she has an inner core of strength. Each day, she grows in confidence."

"Yes," Martinos agreed. *"Although, how do we persuade her to stay with us for longer? We must work to help our people recover. I made a promise to Father."*

"You have grown honor during my banishment. I approve of your intentions. We should make things right for those who depend on us."

Martinos paused, his heart beating faster than average. His

dragon's words pleased him greatly. The support. It would make his job of aiding his people more straightforward.

"Any ideas of how to persuade Cherry to wait for a few more months?"

"I will think," his dragon promised.

Martinos strode alongside Leo and Blaze while their women walked arm-in-arm in front of them. The two chattered in indistinct voices, and Martinos caught laughter too. The pair had chatted non-stop whenever they were together. Martinos turned to Leo. "What will you and Liza do now?"

"We will try again to retrieve Joanna. Eventually, we aim to settle on my farm and stay there where Liza and Joanna are safe from her ex-husband. Her sister will inform their father of his kin's safety."

"You are welcome to stay at the mansion for as long as you wish," Martinos said. "I owe you and Liza my life."

Leo sighed. "I can't do nothing. I must stay busy."

"Help me to re-establish the village and the mansion. Make it productive, more like the village on Hissing Isle. I wish to work with my people rather than issue commands. Our island requires a way to earn money, one we can all benefit from and share. Nandag destroyed the pottery business my mother and her father and grandsire built. There is nothing left. The damage to the oven is extensive, and the experienced tradesmen have disappeared. Cherry told me I should start again, but do things differently so everyone prospers."

"Is that what you truly want?" Leo asked, his gaze hard as if he didn't wholly believe Martinos.

"The lack of freedom and losing my dragon has changed my mindset. It made me evaluate what I had and my past actions. The residents of the village you sent me to treated me as an equal and freely shared what little they had. I can do nothing less." He frowned as his mind slid to Henry and his fishing boat. "Henry was having trouble finding fish to sell and feed his family. I wondered if he'd want to set up a base here. We have no fishing boats. Our people fish from the rocks."

Leo stared at him before giving a slow nod of assent. Martinos felt as if he'd passed a test.

"The number of residents in my local village continues to grow, yet my parents refuse to allow expansion. The younger humans, especially, will welcome a chance to start over on Smoking Isle."

"There might be youngsters on Perfume Isle who will want to relocate too," Blaze said.

"Thank you. I'm uncertain of how to start. Leo, could you take charge of that for me? You and Liza? I will give you full authority to choose a new site if the current position of the village doesn't suit."

"We will work together," Leo stated and extended his hand.

Martinos accepted the handshake with alacrity. This was an excellent first step. "Thank you. I understand my reputation precedes me, and you have doubts, but I promise I am committed to helping my people and supporting my mate."

"Liza," Leo called. "The monastery is over this hill. No more talking please."

Liza waved at Leo and placed her finger to her lips with a nod of understanding. She and Cherry kept walking but slowed their pace to an amble for him and Leo to catch them. He led the way through the undergrowth—bushes with bright yellow flowers and seed pods that clung to Martinos's trews. The winding path led into a grove of oak trees, the leaf litter underfoot, making stealth more difficult.

The five continued in a single file until the tree cover ended. They halted in a tight knot and peered into the open space between them and the hilltop above.

Recently cleared, judging by the scythed piles of grass. The druids had planted the hillside with fruit trees.

"Can you see anyone?" Leo asked.

Martinos scanned the hilltop first, seeing nothing but tall grasses, blackberry thickets, and two mature oaks. "Nothing out of place."

"I can't see or hear a thing," Blaze murmured.

"Anyone?" Leo said. "My gut is rumbling a warning. My senses don't agree."

"It's too quiet," Martinos said.

Leo gave a curt nod and reached out his hand to Liza. "Stay close," he murmured.

Cherry sidled nearer to Martinos, and tucked her fingers into the waistband of his trews, her proximity a comfort to him.

"One of us could shift and do a flyover," Blaze suggested.

Martinos scrutinized the band of fruit trees, the piles of dried grass, and did a slow pass over the crest of the hill. Not an object or person drew his attention, yet apprehension sizzled through him. Leo was right. There was something off, yet his examination of the scene told him nothing.

"A flyover might alert the druids to our presence," Liza murmured.

"We should post a sentry to watch the comings and goings from the monastery," Cherry suggested.

"Our mate is intelligent," Martinos's dragon said.

"Thank you," Cherry replied sweetly. *"That means the world to me."*

"Oh, sarcasm. Cherry, sunbeam, you make my heart go pitter-patter. I love you."

"Later," Martinos said. *"Stay alert, both of you."*

"Blaze, you shift, but don't fly over the ridge yet. Stay with us," Leo said.

Blaze nodded and peeled off his trousers.

"I'll take them for you," Cherry said.

Martinos watched as she turned in Blaze's direction and thrust out her hand but kept her gaze lowered.

"I'll get them," Martinos said, laughter in his voice.

"I can't get used to naked males wandering around," Cherry said.

"The only naked male you should watch is me," Martinos said before his dragon had a chance to add his input.

"You're the only one who draws my attention," she whispered.

While they'd spoken, Blaze had shifted to his dragon, his green hide holding a blue tinge in the light.

"Everyone ready?" Leo asked.

"Yes," Martinos said, his gaze skimming the area in front of them yet again. "Stay close," he murmured to Cherry.

Blaze waited where they'd stopped to reconnoiter while Martinos followed Leo and Liza. Cherry walked at Martinos's side. Each of them hustled toward the nearest fruit tree since the walking was easier near the trees.

Beside him, Cherry stood on a stick. A loud *crack* broke the silence. A pheasant released a startled cry and burst from a nearby thicket.

Everyone froze, waiting.

"I'm so sorry," Cherry said through their mind link.

"Not your fault, sunbeam."

A sharp tug on Martinos's leg had him glancing down. A root pushed from the ground and twirled around his ankle. He tugged free of the questing stem, but another burst from the grass and attempted to catch his other leg. "Move," he ordered, no longer worrying about making a noise.

Cherry raced at his side, halting abruptly when a root the width of her finger grasped her arm and another glided around one calf.

"What is this place?" Liza shouted, frantically yanking at the roots restricting her movement.

"They're only in this area," Martinos said. "Stay away from the fruit trees. Quick, Cherry. Move." He ripped a vine from his leg and plucked another one attempting to wind around Cherry's thigh.

Blaze took to the sky and aimed fire at the area around the base of the fruit tree. A pained whimper assaulted their ears, and the roots subsided, disappearing into the ground as fast as they'd emerged.

"Everyone well?" Leo demanded.

"That was creepy," Liza muttered.

"Yeah," Cherry agreed. "You have plenty of material for when you start to write fiction."

Liza pulled a face. "Tell me about it."

Leo forged a path through the long grass, keeping well away from the juvenile fruit trees. Liza, Cherry, and Martinos followed in that order, while Blaze hovered above them, ready to blast danger with his fire.

"By Lodar," Leo muttered, coming to a dead halt.

Martinos lifted his gaze to the rim of the hill. "There must be at least fifteen druids."

"This looks ominous," Liza whispered.

Cherry's gasp whistled through her teeth. "I don't have a great feeling about this."

As one, the figures in red robes raised their hands. A chant broke the haunting silence, echoing across the land. The hair at the back of Martinos's neck stood on end, and he edged closer to Cherry.

Beside him, Leo sucked in a deep breath and exhaled slowly.

"What are they doing?" Cherry whispered.

As the chanting continued, balls formed at the druids' feet. Martinos stared. *No, not balls.* They were rocks.

"What do they need rocks for?" Liza asked, leaning forward slightly to better see.

The chant grew faster, frenzied, and the rocks multiplied in size until they hid the druids and their red robes.

"By Lodar," Martinos swore as one rock pitched forward until the druid regained control, and the boulder wobbled back into line. Foreboding burst inside Martinos. A stark fear as his mind raced and came to the only possible conclusion.

"Run, sunbeam!" he shouted. "Run as fast as you can toward the oak trees."

Martinos scrambled from his trews just as the druids released their weaponry. The rocks rolled down the hill toward them, gaining momentum.

Cherry and Liza sprinted away while Martinos summoned his dragon. At his side, Leo didn't bother removing his clothing. His dragon burst from him, much faster than Martinos managed.

The rocks gathered speed, racing down the side of the hill. The red robes strode in the wake of their weapons, their magic controlling the sarsens. Their chants continued, growing even louder until the words buzzed in his ears.

Meanwhile, the gigantic rocks tumbled closer and closer.

By Lodar, he wasn't going to make it. *"Hurry,"* he pleaded with his dragon. His dragon slid over him, his scales clicking into place just as Cherry tripped.

Martinos roared and flung his body into the air as the massive boulder passed him, heading directly for Cherry. She pushed to her hands and knees, then scrambled to her feet, glancing over her shoulder as she ran. She darted to the right, and the stone corrected its path, following her.

Blaze attacked the boulder with his fire, and Martinos swooped down, talons extended to pluck Cherry to safety. He managed to hook her jacket enough to raise her off the ground while Blaze breathed fire at the row of druids.

He flew the short distance to the stand of oak trees and set Cherry down with Liza.

The women fell into each other's arms, their breaths coming in ragged pants. Leo and Martinos and finally Blaze joined them. The druids ceased their chanting, and a preternatural silence fell, not even an insect stirring.

Martinos reached for Cherry, both he and his dragon desperate for physical contact. He wrapped his arms around her and breathed in her scent, his heart still beating way too fast. Martinos promised himself he'd work hard to regain his fitness because

Cherry's safety depended on him.

"I'm sorry, sunbeam," he whispered along their private channel.

She seemed to read his thoughts and went straight to the heart. *"You didn't fail me, Martinos. I love you. We're safe and together. That's all that matters. The rest we'll tick off our list, one item at a time."*

"I love you, sunbeam. So much. If we'd lost you..."

"You didn't," she replied. *"Don't borrow trouble."*

Cherry straightened and turned in Martinos's embrace to face Leo, Liza, and Blaze. She peered through the oak trunks at the enormous boulders lined up in a menacing row.

The red robes had vanished, yet the eerie silence remained.

Cherry gulped and ripped her gaze away from the unmoving rocks that were, nonetheless, threatening.

Then, she focused on her mate and her friends. "We're gonna need a better plan."

Want More Cherry?

Not quite ready to let Martinos and Cherry go? Yeah. Me neither. Get a glimpse of their happily ever after as entrepreneurs in the bonus epilogue!

Visit this website to get your free bonus scene: https://dl.bookfunnel.com/5rl9l5dpbfr

Continue the adventure...

Are you ready to read Rena's story next? This feisty varsity student is about to become the main character of her own real-life adventure story.

Visit my website (https://shelleymunro.com/books/rena/) to get your copy of *Rena, Dragon Isles 3,* and read the last book in this trilogy today! Learn what happens to Liza, Cherry, and Liza's half-sister Rena in the final Dragon Isles escapade.

About Shelley

USA Today bestselling author Shelley Munro lives in Auckland, the City of Sails, with her husband and a cheeky Jack Russell/mystery breed dog.

Typical New Zealanders, Shelley and her husband left home for their big OE soon after they married (translation of New Zealand speak - big overseas experience). A twelve-month-long adventure lengthened to six years of roaming the world. Enduring memories include being almost sat on by a mountain gorilla in Rwanda, lazing on white sandy beaches in India, whale watching in Alaska, searching for leprechauns in Ireland, and dealing with ghosts in an English pub.

While travel is still a big attraction, these days Shelley is most likely found in front of her computer following another love - that of writing stories of contemporary and paranormal romance and adventure. Other interests include watching rugby (strictly for research purposes), cycling, playing croquet and the ukelele, and curling up with an enjoyable book.

Visit Shelley at her Website

https://shelleymunro.com

Join Shelley's Newsletter

https://shelleymunro.com/newsletter

Also By Shelley

Paranormal

Middlemarch Shifters
My Scarlet Woman
My Younger Lover
My Peeping Tom
My Assassin
My Estranged Lover
My Feline Protector
My Determined Suitor
My Cat Burglar
My Stray Cat
My Second Chance
My Plan B
My Cat Nap
My Romantic Tangle
My Blue Lady
My Twin Trouble

My Precious Gift

Middlemarch Gathering
My Highland Mate

My Highland Fling

My Elusive Mate

My Valiant Princess

My Highland Wedding

Dragon Investigators
Blue Moon Dragon

Blood Moon Dragon

Black Moon Dragon

Snow Moon Dragon

Dragon Isles
Liza

Cherry

Rena

Sasha